NAME Tammy

HAIR Red. Not a cool, ~~~~ red dye-job. Just plain old carroty brown.

EYES Green or grey depending on my mood.

HOME Above the shop. Small and embarrassing

FAMILY Me, Mum, Dad, baby Mikey. Small and embarrassing.

LOVES Johnny Saunders!!!! Dance class (but not as much as Johnny Saunders), my friends (almost as much as JS, but in a different way), tennis (I think)! Horses and learning to ride!

E-MAIL Tammysjournal@obrien.ie (This is a new one. Don't ask me what the old one was, I'd *die*.)

JUDY MAY grew up in Dublin and is an international traveller and adventurer. She has visited over thirty different countries and has lived in Kathmandu, Paris and New York. She has a degree in Drama and a Masters in literature from Trinity College, Dublin. She loves riding horses and even learned the rodeo art of barrel racing from her cowgirl friends in Texas.

COPPER GIRL

JUDY MAY

THE O'BRIEN PRESS
DUBLIN

First published 2006 by The O'Brien Press Ltd,
12 Terenure Road East, Rathgar, Dublin 6, Ireland.
Tel: +353 1 4923333; Fax: +353 1 4922777
E-mail: books@obrien.ie
Website: www.obrien.ie

ISBN-10: 0-86278-990-7
ISBN-13: 978-0-86278-990-9

British Library Cataloguing-in-Publication Data
May, Judy
Copper girl
1. Teenagers - Fiction 2. Stablehands - Fiction 3. Young adult fiction
I. Title
823.9'2[J]

1 2 3 4 5 6 7 8 9 10
06 07 08 09 10 11 12

The O'Brien Press
receives assistance from

the arts
council
schomhairle
ealaíon

Printed and bound in the UK by CPI Group

For Marguerite Doherty and Deirdre
Doherty, the bravest young girls I know.

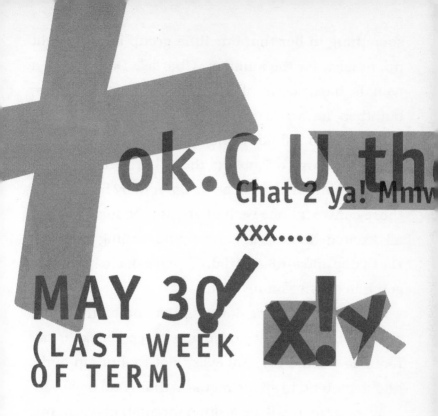

ok.C U th

Chat 2 ya! Mmw

xxx....

MAY 30
(LAST WEEK OF TERM)

I wish I was international, you know, jet set and everything. That way I could be booking a plane ticket somewhere and not just sitting in the bedroom I've had for the past fourteen years re-reading my text messages. 'Chat 2 ya! Mmwah! CU xxx'; that's all it said, like she was going off to dance class and I'd see her after!

I was minding the shop when it first came through and I was so angry I almost threw the phone at the Pringles display. I thought that it should *mean* something to her that our little group is being split up, at least for the summer. Charlie's Dad is *such* a pain; he hasn't even called her much since Christmas, but then he sends for her to join him in Canada without even thinking that she might have a life. What pisses me off most is that Charlie didn't seem to care about months of being ignored by him and all those conversations we had about it, instead she got all excited about Vancouver and sailing and her Dad's dog and stuff and didn't even ask me how I was going to survive on my own.

I spent this evening downstairs minding the shop, pretending to study and dying to get back to my room so I could cry. My eyes kept welling up and I had to pretend to all the regulars that I had hayfever.

At least Hellie will be around for another week, but then it's worse because she doesn't expect to be back *EVER*. She's another one who could work a bit harder at being upset! You'd swear all this was normal. And it's worst for me because I'll be doing the same things as usual except on my own. They'll be having real adventures and meeting amazing people.

They are the best friends I've ever had and at fifteen I'm way too old for getting new ones. I can't think of one other person I know who I could stand for more than a minute-and-a-half.

I don't want Mum to hear me crying in case she thinks it's about Gran and gets all upset herself. I mean, I *am* still upset about that, but I find I can only really cry about one thing at a time, otherwise I get all confused, and the tears stop, and I just feel a more muddy kind of awful.

I have started writing this because last night I saw a film about a girl who found a diary that a girl wrote two hundred years ago and it was *really* interesting. Maybe this will be interesting in the twenty-third century, because God knows there is nothing good about my life right now. In fact the best thing is Johnny Saunders and I only ever walk past him at the bus stop and don't even say anything. Next week I won't even have that, because the exams will be over.

Maybe I should explain about cars and microwaves and iPods and all that, but I suppose they will have better history books in two centuries time, so they won't need those kinds of details from me. I would *love* it if I was important or did something like a really historical person.

LONONGERE
ONG REDNO
ONGCREE
ONGCRE
ONGCRE
1 JUNE

OK, I need to find a bright side or I will go mental. Well, one good thing: I finally know that Johnny *definitely* knows my name. I know this because Hellie met him in her maths grind last night and said, 'I won't see my friend Tammy for ages,' and he said, 'Is she the skinny one with the long red hair and huge green eyes?' and Hellie said, 'Yes.' Which is good for her because usually she would have said something to help that would have made a mess of everything. Also the end-of-term tests were not *complete* torture. Also, Dad said I could use his computer to e-mail Charlie in Canada.

I have to choose a new on-line name, as my old one

is *so* embarrassing that I won't even write it here. I don't even have a good real-life name like Charlie does – I read in a magazine that guys love it when a girl has a tomboy name like Sammie or Nick or Freddie. Last year I tried to get everyone to call me Tommy instead of Tammy, but no one did and Mum gave out to me for confusing the baby. I don't know what web name to use, I just know that it <u>won't</u> have the words 'princess' or 'diva' in it – those are *so* overused.

Mum and I watched some stupid TV show together after she closed up. We hadn't done that since Gran died, so I am feeling a bit happier now and I'm going to bed early to be rested for my English and Science tests in the morning. Dad stayed up making calls until late in the spare-room office because of the new project his business is working on.

6 JUNE
(FIRST WEEK OF MY HOLIDAYS!)

Dance class finished for the summer last night so I'll have to find some other way to exercise (and have a reason to not to do stuff for Mum!) Because it was the last class, we did all the routines we worked on this year, and it was brilliant fun. I love the parts that involve a bit of acting, like pretending to be tough or flirty. I even managed to do a double turn; I didn't get the head bit of that right, but I was still *so* thrilled that I finally got it. It would have been great if Mum or Dad had seen it. I wish the dance school would have a show or something – I'd love that.

After class I went round to Hellie's with her, but couldn't stay long as they were packing up the final bits and pieces into the camper vans (they have these two really cool, old, hippy vans). We both cried and she promised to send postcards. All her family came into the garden to say goodbye and when I asked her dad if they were coming back he said they had to be 'true to the gods of chance and adventure', and might end up anywhere. I wish my dad was more like that, I swear my dad has it worked out where he will be on the planet every day for the rest of his life and what time he'll be having tea. Hellie's older brother gave me a lift back on his bike, and now I don't know when I'll see her again ...

Today we went to visit the grave and Dad brought the garden clippers with him; I only stayed for a couple of minutes for the prayer and then minded Mikey off in the park across from the cemetery. Mum stayed even longer while the rest of us got back in the car, and when she got back her eyes were totally puffy even though she was smiling at us. God, there's been so much crying in our house what with me, Mum and Mikey. Mikey has the best excuse because he's only two-and-a-half. I offered to mind the shop because I knew my Dad was about to ask me to anyway. I don't see why they don't just hire Mr O'Grady to do more hours.

It was mad busy for the first while and then, just as it got quiet, my friend Pete called in. Pete had just dumped his latest girlfriend and I told him to make sure that the next one had a brain bigger than your average orange! I'm secretly glad though, because at least he can hang out with me in town now, and go to Club Havana without some idiot girl giving him grief. Problem is, he's such a laugh that they're falling over him at every opportunity. If he wasn't two years older than me and *totally* unable to have a serious conversation I might even fancy him myself.

I don't even think of him in that way when I think all hope is gone with Johnny, and that's saying something as I sometimes think I'd go out with *anyone* just to have a boyfriend.

Anyway, Pete sat down in his usual place beside the Danishes; he had some new album by one of the bands he loves that no one else has ever heard of, and we listened to it through one earpiece each. I know I'm not supposed to, but I took a Mars Bar and we halved it; I figured I might as well not be a complete slave. Then it got busy again, it being a Lotto day.

10 JUNE
(END OF FIRST WEEK OF HOLIDAYS)

Another day minding Mikey and restocking shelves in the shop. Thrillsville. Now that I have a diary I *have* to do something big or my head will fall off. I solemnly swear that by the end of the summer I will have:

1. Met a rock star or a film star and had a proper conversation with them.

2. Started going out with one of the Rat Pack guys, preferably Johnny Saunders.

3. Got myself on television doing something non-embarrassing.

4. ANYTHING that no one I know has ever done, just to stick it to Adie O'Boyle and her lot.

Once I do that Johnny will really notice me and I'll finally get to go out with him, or even maybe one of the other Rat Pack guys if I decide I'm too big for him. The look on Johnny's face if he asked me out and I turned him down, that would be priceless! Then I will send Hellie and Charlie a really casual e-mail and tell them all about it like as if it's nothing. Yeah, I wish.

Pete laughs at the Rat Pack guys (Hellie came up with the name from some old musicians her dad likes) – he calls them snobs and says they aren't worthy to lick his boots, so I remind him he only ever wears sneakers. I think he's just jealous of Johnny and his friends because they are all from rich families and are *impossibly* good-looking and go to a better school than him. It's a pity because if he was friends with them I'd find it easier to get to know them and wouldn't only say three sentences to Johnny on the odd Friday night at the Club. I was thinking of telling Pete about how much I want to go out with Johnny, but I know he'd just make my life hell about it. Sometimes he acts like my big brother, which is mostly OK.

Right, I am now going to dress in something cool and get into town before 3pm and make something happen. I will get inspired and make a plan or maybe even meet someone and have a life-changing conversation.

LATER

I didn't get into town until five because Mum made me tidy my room first. So it's *entirely* her fault that *all* the interesting people on the planet had gone home by then leaving only Adie O'Boyle and her gang, and Pete and his ex-girlfriend, who was trying to get back with him and kept shooting me dirty looks.

12 JUNE

I woke up at 6a.m. because I forgot to close the curtains last night and the sun came streaming in. I decided to wear my blue t-shirt with the faded jeans and my converse. I did my hair in a couple of little pigtails to try and make it look like something other than just long and straight.

I spent half an hour writing to Charlie and Hellie and then read a book for a while. It's really cool, all about a girl my age who speaks lots of languages and gets to help foil an international smuggling ring. Next year I will pay more attention in German class now that I have a reason! I wonder if you can do espionage as a degree? I guess they'd have to call it something else, so no-one would know. I'll ask Dad if I can learn to ski too, but that would involve money so I know he'll say no. I sometimes fantasise that I'm older and can ski and ride horses and ice-skate and play tennis, and all Adie's lot and the Rat Pack are trying to be my friends, but I have other, better friends who own helicopters. Ridiculous, I know, but I can't help it.

Dad asked me to mind the shop again so he could take Mum and Mikey to the doctors for Mikey's check-up. He can't walk properly because his feet are a bit funny, and so they need to get it sorted. He's so cute though with his tufty auburn baby-hair and the way he laughs all the time as he waddles around. He's the only person in the world I get hugs from these days.

Mum won't let me wear any of what she calls my 'weird stuff' when I'm working. As *if* people would change their minds about wanting a carton of milk and a newspaper just because I'm wearing a shirt with a Japanese cartoon and have three earrings in each ear. I don't mind looking after the shop, I just hate the way they *tell* me rather than ask me, and the way it's always so last minute. Like as if I don't have my own life. Actually, now that the girls are gone, I don't, but they still shouldn't presume.

Then when they got back from the doctor's I thought I could do something like go to the library and that's when Dad handed me a *huge* bag of dry cleaning to bring up to the laundry place. It's half a mile away and I don't have a bike or anything, and as I took the bag Dad said something about my face, about my having an attitude. God, I hate him. I know for a fact that he spent every summer as a teenager swimming, fishing, rock-climbing and playing golf with homemade golf clubs with Uncle Paul. I might ask him to tell me that story again later tonight, just to remind him.

On my way back from the cleaners there was this old lady who was struggling with loads of laundry bags so I asked her if I could help. She was tiny and smiley and had white hair tied up on the back of her head with a purple gem clasp. She was well dressed for an old lady; you know the way some of them dress for comfort or as if they are still in the era they liked best, well she looked really classic and she didn't have a million Kleenexes hanging out her sleeve.

Luckily she only lived nearby because those bags weighed a *ton*, it was like she had just got her armchairs dry cleaned or something! Mrs Miggs (weird name, I know) invited me in for a cup of tea. I actually really needed it at this stage, and plus,

I was in no mood to go home, so I said yes. She had all these pictures of horses everywhere, and her house smelled of lavender, but not in a spray air-freshener way. (Our house always smells of rice for some reason.) When I asked her about the horses she told me this really cool story about how she got her first horse when she was seventeen. First we had to pour the tea as Mrs Miggs said, 'You need tea to oil a good tale.'

She had been helping her mother wash the front step and polish the door when a beautiful chestnut horse just arrived, trotting along with its saddle half hanging off. She ran after the horse and tried to catch it; it was running so fast that it took her a while to notice this young man who was running behind, all irate looking. So, by now she'd caught the horse by the bridle, and the man thanked her and asked her to help him to get the horse back to his father's stables, because he'd hurt his leg in the fall. Her mother looked at her disapprovingly (I know that look so well!), but she went anyway. When they got to the stables, the young man's father started to yell at them both for the state of his magnificent horse. The young man explained to his father that he had to borrow the carriage horse because his own horse was too afraid of the trains to make the trip across

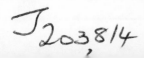

the tracks and over to the sports ground. His father yelled at him even more and told him that he had exactly one day to find a new home for that useless old nag who cost him a fortune in oats and hay.

The young man had nowhere to put his own nervous grey horse and so she (young Mrs Miggs) said he could keep it in her back garden while his father calmed down. She spent the summer meeting up with the young man in the lane and sneaking into the garden to feed the horse and ride it before her parents woke up; they were fine about the horse, not so fine about the man.

I was so into the story that I was surprised to see someone else in the room.

'Has Granny been telling you her "horse and hand" story?' This really tall, giggly girl, about my age, with black hair in a shoulder-length bob, went over and gave Mrs Miggs a hug and then gave out to her for fetching the laundry bags. Mrs Miggs explained that I had helped and the girl grinned at me. She had the most teeth I had ever seen in one person, a bit like a horse herself, but good looking. She smelled like a farm, but not the worst bits of a farm.

'I heard about the horse, but not about a hand,' I said. I hate how I always blush in front of new people, but no one noticed, or at least they didn't say anything.

'Well, by the end of the summer my grandad had asked for Granny's hand in marriage,' the girl said as she poured herself a cup and reached for a slice of cake, 'That's why we call it the "horse and hand" story.'

She then looked me up and down and said that she loved my style, and Mrs Miggs said, 'Yes, indeed, very unique.'

I felt my face burning and felt really silly and out of place so I mumbled that I had to be back home and they both said to drop in anytime.

I think I look ordinary, even though I wear arty clothes. I bet people can tell that I'm ordinary, all dressed up with no place to go, and all that. I don't care, I like my clothes, and my friends think I look good too. It's only Adie and Doris who ask me if I made that outfit myself, but they are professional bitches and it's their job.

Sometimes when I look at Adie sneering at me, I can't believe that we used to be best friends. We met when we were four at our first day at kindergarten and she used to be round at my house all the time – until we were nine and Doris joined the school and took Adie out on her Dad's boat and then that was it. I remember Mum kept asking where Adie was and I couldn't think what to say, and then she eventually stopped asking. It was another year before I became friends with Charlie and Hellie and I can't *believe* that Adie let me sit on my own at lunch (or with other groups of friends who would be a bit confused as to why I was sitting with them) for all that time. She didn't start to get really, really horrible until I had new friends, but we decided early on not to stoop to their level although we are just as bitchy behind their backs, which means I'm not as brilliant as I pretend to be.

The whole thing is really stupid and it means I sometimes can't get to talk to Johnny Saunders because I don't want her to see me talk to him because she and Doris would tell him horrible things about me. One time after I got an A for an English essay and they got Ds and the teacher had me read it out at assembly, they told everyone that I had a verruca on my foot and that's why they couldn't invite me to their pool party.

That girl at Mrs Miggs's looked amazing, not pretty and over-groomed like Adie and Doris, but like she could be a model when she's older, really different. I bet she rides horses and sails boats and all the things the rich girls and the Rat Pack guys do.

Dad yelled at me for not being home on time because it meant he had to pay the childminder extra. I said 'take it out of my wages', but not loud enough for him to hear.

I didn't get upset because I kept imagining Mrs Miggs's story. It must have felt *so* good, smuggling carrots and oats through to the back field with the guy she ended up marrying. You see, all the good stuff happened in history. Nothing good goes on these days, everyone is too busy.

13 JUNE

Today was weird. My school report arrived in the post this morning so I legged it, gulped down some cornflakes, put my head around my parents' bedroom door to say 'I'm off', and was out the door to give them time to get over my being not *quite* the wunderkind they had hoped for. It's not as if it's ever really bad, but it's so full of Bs and 'could do betters' that I get a big lecture from both of them and have to make promises about concentrating more and being more responsible so I can get into medicine and blah, blah, blah ...

I didn't have any money so I decided to hang out on the bench at the back of the railway bridge. It's nice there and no one bothers you. I was a bit pissed off when I got there because someone else had obviously had the same idea as me, but then I was glad when I saw it was Mrs Miggs's granddaughter, the tall girl from yesterday.

She gave me this impossibly big smile and said, 'School report just arrived, I had to escape Granny's thinly-veiled disappointment, and my friends are all away for the summer so I ended up here.'

'You're lucky having the thin veil, my folks' disappointment comes out blazing,' I said, blushing again for absolutely no reason whatsoever, 'My name's Tammy by the way.'

'Marianne,' she said, 'God, I bet I failed everything. It doesn't help that my brother Martin is only two years older than me and only gets As, like he's allergic to anything else.'

I told her that I loved her Granny's story about the horses, and she told me that horses were a family thing. Her parents had kept horses, which were passed on to her and her brother Martin. I wanted to ask her what had happened to her parents, but I didn't feel like I knew her well enough. She said she'd been late going to help with the laundry bags yesterday because they'd had some trouble at the stables (which explains the farm smell). I thought she was going to say that a horse had lost a shoe or someone left a gate open, but it turned out to be much bigger.

Her grin got a little smaller as she told me the whole story.

'My parents built the stables when they were first married. There are only ten horses there at the moment, four belong to me and Martin, and six are owned by other people who pay us rent, and that money keeps the whole thing going. And it's been that way for three years without any bother. The manager stayed on for the first year and then we just did it all ourselves. Martin does the money stuff. He's been amazing with money ever since he was a really small boy.

'The only problem is that now there's this neighbour who doesn't even live all that near, who wants to close us down. He's been saying for months that we're a health hazard, a security risk, that we break noise pollution laws ... anything he can think of to get rid of us. He's really rich so he has his lawyers send us letters. We just stick them under an old tack-box and ignore them! But the other morning we were mucking out and this local government man showed up in a suit and handed us a piece of paper saying we had eight weeks to close the place down and find new homes for all the horses, because they had discovered that the 'facility' was being run by underage workers and other rubbish like that. Martin went mental, started waving his pitchfork at the man, shouting at him to get off our land, all very dramatic. Granny is the registered owner of the stables, even though Martin and I really run it, but we don't bother her with any of the problems; she has enough on her plate just raising us.'

'What will happen if you can't find new homes for the horses?' I asked, feeling slightly miffed that our back garden is only just big enough to hold a swing, a tree and a birdbath.

'Well,' Marianne said, looking like she might cry, 'Let's just say we *have* to. My brother Martin insists that we spend our time fighting the decision to close us down, and finding a way to get them on legal or business terms. He spends every waking hour doing research on the internet and stuff, but I'm scared that if we spend our time doing that and we lose, then we won't have time to find them new homes and save their lives. He's got such a business head that sometimes he doesn't see the wood for the trees.'

Then Marianne decided that she should go to the stables to make calls to the other owners letting them know what was happening.

'I've been too angry to do it until today,' she

grinned. She is so relaxed and balanced that I find it hard to believe she could get angry.

I wanted to ask if I could go with her, but I've never been to a stables before and I was too afraid in case I got there and made a fool of myself. I wasn't keen on the idea of meeting her brilliant-but-mad brother Martin with the pitchfork either! She gave me her phone number though, and said we could meet up again really soon.

I hung around for ages after, but was starving by lunchtime and so I left the bench and went back to brave the results.

I got all Bs (big surprise) and every single teacher said I could get As if I wanted to. I think I'll do worse next time, get Cs to get them off my back for the next three years.

Dad sighed loudly and said he's disappointed in me. Well I'm disappointed in him too, I'm pissed off that he doesn't make enough money so that Mum can be a mum, and I can be a teenager. Mum only cares that I'm around to be free slave labour in the shop and a free babysitter. Dad hasn't minded the shop himself in about two years, it's so easy for him just to escape to his office and have me do everything. I sometimes think he's playing computer games in there and not really starting a new business at all.

14 JUNE

Today I did nothing, so much for my exciting new life. I just minded the shop for the morning and Mikey for the afternoon and he mostly watched tots' TV, which had all these overly happy twenty-year-olds talking like simpletons to kids and wearing clothes the colours of sweet wrappers. I am starting to know all the songs and hand gestures, which is a worry. I did his physiotherapy exercises with him and he was really brave.

I bet Charlie and Hellie did amazing things today on their foreign adventures. I bet Pete even met a new girl. He hasn't dropped in, and that's fairly ominous. I hope the new one is a cow so I have a built-in excuse not to talk to her much. Sometimes they think they have to suck up to me and sometimes they think they have to make Pete go off me. I will have to do cool things tomorrow so I don't have to lie and make up stuff when I e-mail the girls.

I still haven't forgiven Dad for not letting me go travelling with Hellie. I could have just gone for the first two weeks even, on the French bit, it's not like I had to follow them right across Europe. They all wanted me to go and I would have finally, for the first time in my life, got a tan. I bet if they had been going places Dad could pronounce he'd have felt very different about the whole thing. It's not like we ever go on holiday ourselves thanks to Dad's business ventures. Before I go to bed I will write a poem so at least it won't have been a wasted day.

15 JUNE

The poem I wrote was pathetic enough to be hilarious. I know that 'money' and 'sunny' do *not* really rhyme with 'Johnny', but in English half the poets didn't even bother their arses getting that far. Anyway I'm not really the kind of person who writes poetry, it was really a bunch of lyrics, which are easier because you can just repeat the good bits endlessly, assuming there are any good bits.

Imagine Johnny Saunders knew I had written a poem about him. I'd *die*. Christ, imagine *anyone* knew. It will be all right when people read this in the twenty-third century though, because at that stage no one will have written a poem for a century-and-a-half and they'll think I'm a genius, especially for the way I compared his hair to several small bits of seaweed. 'Seaweed' and 'my need' also sort of rhymes. It does too, Your Honour!

TOMORROW

CLUB HAVANA

20 JUNE

I called Marianne and asked her if she was going to the under-eighteens dance at Club Havana. She got really excited and said she'd never been there and had always wanted to go because her brother Martin always went, but never took her with him. It was fun to see her so excited as she is really laid back and seems to take most things in her stride. I really don't like the sound of this brother. We were on the phone forever as I told her all about the other times I'd been there and what sort of thing to wear and who to avoid and look out for.

Anything might happen tomorrow night. Johnny should be there. I already told Marianne that there's this guy I fancy and haven't spoken to in six weeks, just in case she accidentally went for him, not knowing. She thinks she knows who Johnny is, but I think she might be confusing him with another blond Rat Pack guy called Sean. Charlie and Hellie and I always had an agreement that we could each like one guy at a time who the others were not allowed to go for. It means that we have never fallen out over a guy.

The thing is, I think Adie O'Boyle fancies Johnny too and they both belong to the tennis club and go to those dances too. I must think of something clever to say and something *amazing* to wear.

21 JUNE

I can't sleep. I don't know if tonight was a failure or a success. Bits of both, I guess. Pete and I called around to Marianne's at seven and we arrived just as her brother Martin was coming downstairs. Pete already knew him, they go to the same school and are both in the photography club. He looks kind of sulky, otherwise he looks pretty much like Pete does, dark hair, tall, and wearing a t-shirt of some band that's so underground they will only ever sell fifty albums. His face is kind of like Marianne's, big blue eyes, large mouth – except without the big grin. He could be good looking if he made the effort.

I was happy to leave them to talk while I went up to

Marianne's bedroom to help her choose which shoes worked best. She looked amazing all dressed up, really classically beautiful and cool, her bobbed black hair looking as smooth and shiny as an ad. We laughed about how different we looked as I was in my most ripped and punky black dress with long buckled boots and my hair gelled and pinned into crazy shapes. I looked great too though, and I don't often say that.

It's only a five-minute walk from their house to Club Havana. I *love* that bit of the night where you walk in and go from it being bright outside to being all dark and really loud and hot. We didn't have to join any line, and when we got in the four of us danced together for a while and then the guys got talking to some other guys while Marianne and I went to walk around to see if Johnny Saunders was there.

He wasn't. So we went back to dance some more and then Martin got us all waters and we sat outside on the patio for a bit. Pete started chatting up this girl who was *almost* wearing a dress, and Marianne got asked to dance by this guy a foot shorter than her, so that left me and Martin talking about who we knew and what films we had seen recently. He wasn't quite so scary, but then he didn't have his pitchfork with him! He was smart and really funny, I bet he thinks he can be as sulky as he likes and then get forgiven just by saying something witty. Then I saw Johnny walk past, so I pretended I needed to go to the bathroom and left Martin sitting there and went back inside.

God, I go all stupid whenever I see Johnny, he is just *so* gorgeous that all I want in life is to run my fingers through that thick, blond hair and to be able to have Adie and her friends and the Rat Pack all see me going out with him. Sometimes I make up scenes in my head about him, I imagine that people say something against me and he sticks up for me.

He (real-life Johnny, not the one in my head) was standing near the second room and I brushed past him on my way and then said, 'Oh, hi!', like I was surprised to see him. He looked kind of pleased to see me too, I think. I asked him about his exams and what he was doing for the summer and I made him laugh a couple of times. Then I noticed Marianne and Martin a few feet away, and they both looked really agitated. Then Martin pushed past Johnny and me, looking like he wanted to punch someone's lights out and Marianne followed and whispered in my ear, 'I have to go.'

Her brother is a *complete* pain. I really hate him.

She was having such a good time in spite of the really short guy. What's the use of being nice one minute if you are going to be a complete psycho the next? Martin needs to sort his head out.

At that stage the rest of the Rat Pack arrived and Johnny went off. I know that if I hadn't got distracted I could have kept him there talking, which had me extra pissed off. Then Pete and I danced again, which was funny and embarrassing as he kept singing the words and miming guitars and drums. Then I was really pissed off when Doris danced with Johnny, so Pete walked me home, talking all the time about how many girls' numbers he had collected. He tried to throw me into a hedge until I took back what I said about the girls not wearing their contact lenses.

God, I had so hoped that Marianne and Pete might get together and I'd get asked out by Johnny and everyone would be happy. Except Martin, who was born to be miserable and deserves it. It *never* works out the way you plan it in your head.

22 JUNE

I called over to Marianne early to make sure we were still friends and she didn't hate the club, or me, or blame me for leaving Martin sitting on his own. She was really happy to see me and I was glad there was no sign of Martin.

'I wanted to make sure that it wasn't anything I did wrong,' I said.

She said, 'I was just coming over to your place to tell you why we left so quickly,' and then stopped because her granny was in the room with us.

While Mrs Miggs was in the kitchen Marianne rapidly explained to me, 'That guy you were talking to, his name is Saunders, right?'

'Yeah, Johnny Saunders,' I said.

'It's his father, Mr Robert Saunders, who is closing down our stables. Martin took one look at him and his blood started to boil, so that's why he left, so there wouldn't be a fight.'

I started to say that I was sure Johnny knew nothing about what his Dad was doing and about the horses being in trouble, but Mrs Miggs came back in with the tea. An hour later, after talking about everything except the things we really wanted to talk about, Marianne walked me up to the end of the road. She said that she'd love to bring me over to the stables, but that Martin was so tetchy these days that she didn't dare without asking him first. They had called a lawyer, but it was going to cost too much money so they were going to have to fight it out alone. I must think of a way to help her. I think they should tell their granny, but Marianne says Martin said 'no way' to that because she's so old.

25 JUNE

Marianne called in while I was minding Mikey, and in between doing the songs (which I can now do without the TV on) to make Mikey laugh, we talked all about guys and about the horses and came up with all kinds of ideas for both. It seems best if I go and talk to Johnny to get him to persuade his Dad to let the stables stay open. That way I get to talk to him and we also get to save the stables. Double win!

Marianne doesn't fancy Pete because although he is tall and fun he has so many other girls on the go, but she really likes him as a friend. I think there are a couple of Rat Pack guys that might suit her.

I know it's really stupid, but I got really

embarrassed when Marianne met my parents. Dad was wearing that jumper with the hole in the elbow, and Mum kept calling her 'Ann-Marie'. I wish I had a genius artistic family like Hellie's. I guess I'm lucky that I have parents. I still haven't asked Marianne what happened to hers, it's not something you can ask casually like, 'By the way, did your parents die in a car crash, or some other way?' I wonder if she visits their grave the way we do with Gran's.

26 JUNE

Martin came into the shop today and I pretended not to notice him until he got to the counter. I felt like I wanted to say something about Johnny not being like his Dad or something. But instead I just said 'Hi' and took the money for the apples. I don't know why he didn't get them at the supermarket where they are much cheaper. He looked broody, (like I expected anything else!) but at least he asked how I was and how Pete was. Just as I was about to be rid of him Pete arrived in and they started to talk about some camera thing that I didn't understand. I overheard Martin say, 'Why don't you come up to the stables and take some pictures of the horses?'

Pete got all excited about that, and then I nearly fell over when Martin turned to me and added, 'You too Tammy, if you're up for it.' I guess he felt he had to, with me standing there.

Pete was as revved-up as a motorbike and arranged for us to go up the next morning.

'I'm there from six a.m.,' Martin said.

Yeah, like I'm going to be out of bed by six a.m.

27 JUNE

At 5.45 a.m. I woke up to a rapping sound on the window. Pete has this way of climbing over our back wall, up onto the roof of the downstairs toilet, and then using the tree to swing onto the stone balcony outside my bedroom. It's not really a balcony that you can use as it's only a few inches deep, but it's wide enough to balance there long enough to annoy me into getting out of bed. He had first done that four years ago when he needed to borrow a flashlight for some fishing thing in the middle of the night, and now he does it every couple of months, usually if he has an idea or problem and can't sleep until he's chatted to someone about it.

This morning he wouldn't go away, so I pulled on a pair of baggy jeans and a sweatshirt over my PJs and then some boots, and met him in the front garden. I always have to let my parents know when I'm leaving the house. When it's this early they're still half asleep even when I wake them, so I always leave a note to say where I am and what time I'll be back. This one said,

'Marianne's place, back at noon,'

That's how I found myself yawning and swatting gnats at stupid o'clock in the morning with the smell of horseshit growing stronger as we walked up the lane to the stables.

It was really amazing, a small, square courtyard with cream-painted, wooden-roofed stone stables on two sides, and a long brick building that looked like an office and a storeroom. There were trees and plants and flowers growing wild here and there and a small white kitten playing with a bridle hanging from one of the stable doors. Some of the dozen or so doors had the top half open, and horses of different colours and sizes were looking out, blinking and moving their heads like as if they were having a conversation.

Martin gave us a quick tour and then he stood with Pete as they looked at camera lenses and things. I was patting the nose of this lovely chestnut-coloured pony (ignoring Pete's jokes about it having the same hair as me) when Martin tapped me on the arm.

'Let's put you to work then,' he actually smiled, and looked like his sister for a second as he handed me a small grooming brush. I was going to argue that I had enough of being the favourite slave at home, but I did really want to get closer to a horse. I don't think I'd ever touched one before today.

Martin opened a stable door further down and said, 'Here, this is Marianne's horse, my sleeping beauty sister's not up yet.' It was a gorgeous white horse called Shine who knew to walk out to the courtyard. Pete took pictures while Martin showed me how to groom her, and then left me to my own devices. After a while Pete went off to click away elsewhere and I kept brushing. I really loved it. I can't remember ever having such a cool time and it was just me and this white horse.

Marianne arrived a while later, and we mucked out a couple of the stables singing all the new chart songs we could remember and sometimes whispering when we wanted to talk about the Rat Pack. I can't believe we've only known each other a couple of weeks. Meanwhile Martin and Pete took all the saddles and bridles and blankets out of the tack room (hey, get me with all the lingo!) and washed it out before putting all the stuff back. Then we all went back to their house where Mrs Miggs made us a huge breakfast of apple porridge, toast, and scrambled eggs and bacon. I couldn't believe it was still only 10.30. It was brilliant, like meals with Hellie's family, everyone laughing and teasing each other and talking over each other. I would love to live there.

I got back around midday and minded the shop, which was so quiet that I got to finish my book. I have an idea for tomorrow so I am getting to bed early tonight. Plus, I'm knackered.

at marianne's again, back at noon

28 JUNE

I left the note in the usual place.

This morning started great. I met Marianne as arranged at the stables at seven. We agreed that somehow that extra hour in bed makes it more civilised. Martin was in the stables office on the internet and didn't bother to come out to say hello. But that was better in a way because it meant he didn't see me get up on Shine for my first lesson. Once we stopped laughing long enough and found a bucket to upturn for me to stand on, I got into the saddle.

Marianne took the reins and we walked down to

the bottom of the lane to an enormous field, which she explained also belonged to them. I kept feeling I was going to fall off even though the horse was only walking slowly, and then after half an hour I felt like I would stay on, but my legs were about to fall off, so we decided to call it a day. The riding-hat really pinched my head so it was a relief to get rid of that, but I felt really proud of myself. As we were grooming and feeding the rest of the horses we were talking and laughing really loudly and Martin emerged from the office at one point and muttered at us to keep the noise down because he was working on something.

My favourite is the dark-chestnut pony, Copper Girl, who is a bit smaller than Shine and belongs to Martin. Marianne told me that he doesn't ride her as much as he rides his other horse, a stunning Arabian stallion called Arab (not much imagination on the horse-naming front then!) I find Arab *way* too frisky and don't go near him much, I'm a bit afraid of him. When Martin saw that I'd groomed and fed Copper Girl he said I could ride her the next time. Marianne liked that idea because then she could ride Shine alongside. Her other horse, a lumbering, black gentle giant called Grimsby Town, is lame so no-one can ride him until he's better. Martin explained that he does the vet's garden for him once every two weeks so he takes care of their horses for free. I reckon maybe Martin is not as bad as I first thought he was, although he is grumpy most of the time and he does always seem to be talking about money or practical things.

Marianne came to my place for breakfast in case they needed me, and she left when I went to go and help Mum with the new deliveries.

Then after stocking the shelves, miracle of miracles, Mum asked me did I want her to mind the shop for a couple of hours if I had stuff to do. I almost said no because Mum looks so tired, but then I remembered my idea about finding Johnny and having that chat. I called Pete, but he was out with this new girl, I always know by his voice when he's with someone. I called Marianne, but her phone went through to voicemail; she's probably calling around to get new homes for the horses. So I went off toward the tennis club, after changing my outfit three times, knowing I'd find Johnny Saunders there.

He was standing in his white shorts and white t-shirt looking amazing, doing practice serves on his own on one of the courts. I was feeling really good and really brave so I just walked over to him and asked him if he had five minutes to talk about something.

I said, 'I don't think you know about this, but two friends of mine own this amazing horse riding stables and if it gets closed down then some of the horses might have to be put down and your Dad is the one who wants it closed so I was wondering if you would talk to him about it.'

I then finally drew breath and realised from the confused look on his face that he hadn't understood a word I'd said. After I explained it all again, slower, he just shrugged and said, 'It's nothing to do with me. My dad is a really powerful business man and I never talk to him about his dealings with small businesses, we mostly just talk about the larger mergers and things.'

And that was that. I could feel myself about to go red again so I said that I just wanted to make sure he knew and then started to walk away. Not brilliant, but OK-ish.

He walked with me to the clubhouse and said I must come and play tennis sometime, which is as close to him asking me on a date as I've got in the last year. I explained that I'm not a member, and he said that I could pick up a form and get my parents to take out a family membership. He was really friendly and smiling, and gave me a membership form on my way out, but I know there's no way we'd ever have that kind of money. I'm pretty sure he held my gaze for a second longer than usual, at least long enough for me to notice that his eyes are brown and not blue like I thought before.

I hope he mentions it to his dad about the stables. Maybe this could all be over by tomorrow and we can just enjoy riding the horses. Maybe Marianne will let me invite Johnny to come riding one day, after I've learned how to keep my feet.

29 JUNE

Rode Copper Girl, tried trotting, backside in bits. Too tired to write.

30 JUNE

I absolutely *love* riding Copper Girl, and can't believe I only started a few days ago. I'm up at six (!!!! crazy stuff, it feels like Christmas every morning and I'm promised Johnny Saunders wrapped up under the tree!) and not back until twelve, just in time to eat before starting at the shop. I rewrite the same note,

'Marianne's – back at noon.'

Today Dad asked, 'Who's Marianne?' He never pays attention to anything to do with me.

This morning was really amazing.

Martin gave me my lesson as Marianne was

teaching Pete on Shine. I found myself trying extra hard because I didn't want him to think I was an idiot. He had me walking Copper Girl with my feet out of the stirrups (just as I had learned to keep them in!) and then even trotting a bit like that, which was pretty scary, but nice-scary. Martin told Marianne I was getting really good, and Marianne told Martin that Pete needs to learn that horses can't be tricked the way some girls can.

Then we all groomed the horses for a while and the atmosphere was really good, everyone was in such a chilled-out place, Martin even joined in the singing! It was pretty hot, so we didn't feel like doing any of the heavy stuff. Instead we went back to the field with Martin when he took Arab out. Marianne and I helped him set up some jumps while Pete ran home for his camera. The rest of the morning Marianne and I just lazed on the grass in the middle of the field, watching Martin jump the jumps around the edges. Pete took pictures for a while then fell asleep beside us. Marianne used a daisy to try to make him snore and I remembered I hadn't told her about talking to Johnny at the tennis club so I quickly filled her in on that. She agrees that his asking me to play tennis is a *very* good sign.

Martin is amazing on a horse; he just kept going

and going, totally focused.

'That's why he's so good at everything,' Marianne said, 'He just keeps going way after anyone else would have given up.'

I wanted to say what a pity it was that he wasn't trying so hard to find new homes for the horses, but didn't want to spoil the ideal moment. After a while Pete woke up and started picking at the grass and throwing it on us, and I realised it was time to go.

I'm going to conjure it all up again as I fall asleep, the sound of the horses' hooves, the look of the grass and trees, Kitten the kitten playing in Marianne's coat, the feel of the cool breeze and the hot sun, the way it felt so good.

1 JULY

I was so excited this morning that I was up even earlier and had time to make myself look like less of a degenerate than the last few times I was at the stables. On the walk there I realised the birds sing so loudly at that time of the morning. I got to the end of the lane just after seven and Marianne was standing there waiting for me, looking anxious, so I presumed that Grimsby Town's leg had got worse.

As soon as she saw me she started to run over.

'Things have backfired,' she said, and moved us off back the way I had just come. I was freaking and she wouldn't tell me anything until we got almost as far as the main road.

'It's going to be OK,' she reassured me, 'It's just that last night, when Martin went to lock up, Mr Saunders showed up and started yelling and ranting at Martin not to involve his son Johnny in things, and calling him every name under the sun. Martin didn't have a clue what he was on about, so he came straight back home, and burst into my bedroom to ask me if I knew anything about it.'

'What did you tell him?'

'I told him about our plan and he lost it completely.'

She then explained that she told Martin that we thought it would work, and that he should be *pleased,* not angry. Anyway, apparently he is so angry with us that it's best to keep out of his way.

'But at least we did *something,* I mean what's he doing about it himself? Looking up laws on the internet won't help!'

Marianne sort of agreed, but said that Martin kept insisting he would handle things himself. She said things would be back to normal in a couple of days, that he always calmed down.

So I had to just go home and spend a boring day there. I tidied my room and made it look really great and then did the same with the living room, which made Mum happy. I even did the windows. At least all this big mess means that Johnny said something to his Dad, that he has a heart and wants to help. Maybe he even did it for me, I mean he did ask me to come and play tennis some time. I wonder if maybe he could have me there as his guest, then I'll only have to save up enough to buy a dress and racket. I could get another job in town in the mornings especially if I can't go to the stables again.

I am *so* pissed off with Martin, throwing his weight around, getting all angry when I was only trying to help. At least I did something, I wasn't afraid to actually talk to someone about it. I want to go up there tomorrow and tell him what I think of him.

2 JULY

I didn't have the courage in the morning, but then I got so annoyed thinking about it all day in the shop that I decided not to let him and his stupid temper push me around. I waited until nine in the evening when I knew Martin would be there on his own, locking up for the night.

He was just leaving as I arrived. Just as expected, he had his sulky face on.

'Look,' I launched in at full volume before he could have a go at me, 'I know you hate me for talking to Johnny ...'

'I don't ...'

'Please, don't interrupt. I know that you care more

about the stables and your business than about actually saving the horses' lives, but I *care* about these horses and I'm prepared to do whatever it takes to save them. I'm not afraid of some stupid businessman and what he thinks I should or shouldn't do. If you weren't so gutless you could have had all this sorted by now.'

I was expecting him to yell back, but instead he looked more stern and said in a low, quiet voice, 'So that's what you think of me, is it?'

'Yes!' I could feel the blood pumping in my hands and face at this stage.

He then turned around and walked away back to the office, and I marched back down the lane feeling triumphant for having finally stood up to him.

I now hate him and always will. I feel sorry for Marianne that she has a brother like that, but I'm determined that it won't affect our friendship.

5 JULY

I didn't go round to the stables for the last few days for obvious reasons. I just lay awake in the mornings feeling sorry for myself and angry with Martin. I didn't even try to get a new money-paying job.

Pete has been up there helping out, and he called into the shop and showed me some of the pictures of me patting Copper Girl and grooming Shine, which he took the first day we went up there. That made me feel worse and so did his new jokes, which made me laugh so much that when I came out of laughing I realised I hadn't laughed in days.

He gave me a message from Marianne saying she'd call in tomorrow, she's just been so busy trying to get the stables in great shape in case that becomes a deciding factor. Apparently she is really worried that I might not want to go over there any more and might not want to be her friend. I'm so lucky to have a new friend like her. I'll head over tomorrow morning and just apologise to Martin for Marianne's sake, although I don't regret one word of what I said, it's best to keep the peace. I don't imagine he'll let me ride Copper Girl any more.

6 JULY

Everything has gone completely wrong! It makes all the other stuff – Gran dying, Charlie and Hellie going away, having to work all the time, the stables closing and the row with Martin – seem like nothing.

Today I was leaving the house at eight o'clock, thinking that Marianne would have got back from her ride so we could muck-out and chat together, when Mum and Dad asked me to come into the living room and sit down. It was exactly like they did when Gran died a few months ago except this time they were smiling. I thought maybe they had decided to get that new car they always talk about but never buy. But they told me that Mum is pregnant, that they are going to have a new baby. I wanted to scream at them. They can't even cope with Mikey and the other stuff without me being there to bail them out. This is *so* selfish of them, now I won't have any time for myself whatsoever. I hate to upset Mum though, because she is so sensitive, so I hugged her and said, 'A new baby, that's great.' I had started to cry a bit, but she must have thought they were tears of happiness and she started to cry too. I just stuck on a grin and pretended I was late to meet someone and ran off saying how great the news was.

A new baby, I can't take it!

I couldn't face going to the stables right then, and I didn't want to be on my own behind the railway bridge so I found myself going to Mrs Miggs's house. I never really got to have a granny because although I really loved my gran, she'd had Alzheimer's since I was little and never knew who I was. I thought I would just go over and have a cup of tea and ask her to tell me the 'horse and hand' story again, but as soon as she opened the door I burst out crying. She gave me a big, long hug saying, 'There, there, little one,' and bustled me in to the living room and sat me on the sofa.

'Tell me all about it,' she said.

She listened attentively as everything came

flooding out about how I hate my Dad for always expecting me to work, and how Mum seems so weak and how I worry about her, and about how I love Mikey, but hate having to look after him all the time. I told her that the new baby would be arriving in six months and my life would be pretty much over from that moment on.

Mrs Miggs is the best. She didn't try and tell me that it would be OK; she just said that when you have people around you who love you, you can cope with anything. That made me cry even more.

'I feel really stupid,' I sniffed, 'because I know that compared to other things, a new baby is a great thing. I just can't help feeling like I do. I'm sorry. You must think I'm really silly and selfish for getting upset.'

'Not in the least,' said Mrs Miggs, 'Things of different kinds happen, and we feel what we need to feel at the time, and then we move on.'

Mrs Miggs left me sitting on the sofa while she went in to put the kettle on. God, she loves to make tea!

As she pottered away in the kitchen I looked around the room, and saw for the first time that on the mantlepiece was a large family portrait in a silver frame. I could recognise Marianne and Martin even though they were around eight and ten in the photograph, and realised that that must be their parents behind them. I lifted it down to take a closer look.

'Gran? Have you seen my long riding boots?' Martin was in the door and striding through the room before I knew what had happened. He suddenly saw me there, holding the huge picture. I went *really* red and didn't know whether to put the picture down or keep holding it. But he mumbled, 'Hi,' more sadly than unpleasantly, and I said 'Hi,' back. He put his hand through his hair in this way he does when he gets flustered and by the time he came back out of the kitchen with his boots I'd put the picture back and got myself together a bit.

'I'm really sorry about the other night,' I mumbled, forcing myself to look him in the eye.

He smiled nervously and said, 'That's OK.' Then he filled the awkward pause by saying, 'The horses miss you, especially Copper Girl. Why don't you come over tomorrow?'

I nodded, and he left.

I feel like a complete bitch for not being nicer to him before. It's his own fault though, he shouldn't be so sulky and so focused on the legal stuff when it's the horses' *lives* he needs to be saving. Anyway, I chatted to his granny about how much fun it is learning to ride, being careful not to mention any trouble. She made me laugh telling me about when her soon-to-be-husband taught her to ride the grey, and how she got in trouble with her mother for stealing a pair of her father's trousers to wear for it.

I caught my reflection in a window as I was leaving and saw that my eyes were all red and my face totally puffy. Martin must think I'm mentally unstable, yelling one day and crying all over the place the next.

I went over to Pete's house and read through his rock magazines while I let my face calm down enough to go home. He played me the same song twenty times, saying, '... this bit, listen to this bit,' every now and then.

Tonight I pretended to go to sleep early so I could cry on my bed. I think I have cried more this summer than all the other summers put together. I feel that Mum and Dad love Mikey and the new baby more than they love me, otherwise they would have considered me and not let Mum get pregnant.

WHADIE
WHY? DORIS
WHY?
7 JULY WHY?

Today I saw Adie and Doris in the last place on the planet I imagined I would. It was like one of those sci-fi futuristic shows where people end up in totally different worlds from where they are supposed to be. I was just returning Copper Girl to her stable while Marianne was out doing some proper riding, cantering and stuff, when I heard Martin laughing in one of the stables and heard those two flirting with him. They never just talk to guys, they always flirt, just like they never talk to me, they always bitch. Coming out of the middle stable on the far side they looked as perfect and wonderful as I knew they would, Adie in cream jodhpurs and a white shirt,

Doris in a short dress, her hair all curled, and both wearing enough make-up to appear in a cheap rock video.

They looked happy to see me at first, but I knew it was an act. They do that, and they say something like, 'I love your outfit, my friend had one just like it a couple of years ago.' So they sound like they are being sweet, but they're really saying that your clothes are out of date. Today Adie looked at my riding hat, one of Marianne's old ones, and said, 'I must bring down my old riding hat for you, Tammy, you'd be much happier with that, although I know you don't really mind about how you look.'

God, I could have killed her. I wished Pete was there, he'd have thought of the best comeback line.

Then she said to Martin and Doris, 'Well, I think I'll just sell Indian, it's not like I even ride him any more since we got the boat.'

Indian is a really nice piebald pony who no-one ever seems to visit, and now I know why.

'I don't suppose you'd like to buy him Tammy?' Doris said, in her fake, sickly-sweet way, 'You could keep him in the shop if you move out the rest of the rubbish.'

They both started to giggle, and I went really red and went over to the tap to get fresh water for

Copper Girl. I hope she does sell Indian, he deserves a better owner than her.

They left pretty soon after that, which was a relief, as we had to muck out Indian's stable. I think Martin went with them, as we didn't see him again all morning.

I wonder if I ever lost my temper with Doris or maybe if I sat down with Adie and had a conversation then they might sign some kind of peace treaty with me? I have a feeling it wouldn't make a difference. It's like they can only feel good about themselves by looking down on me. I might do the same except I seem to be at the bottom of the pile around here!

It was so great to see Marianne who was really in a great mood and she chatted away, asking me questions about the Rat Pack, so I filled her in on each of them in way more detail than before. There are about eight, and she decided that Jeremy sounds best. She is so easy-going and *much* more sensible than me, it makes her so easy to hang out with. We decided to look amazing at the next dance, and to dance near them, but pretend to completely ignore them. We must keep Pete and Martin away in case Johnny and Jeremy think that we have boyfriends.

MY SPACE.

8 JULY

Mum has noticed that I'm not spending the mornings at home, I guess she is missing her free babysitter. I don't know why I'm not telling them about the stables and learning to ride, I suppose I feel that it's something just for me, that no-one can tell me to do or not to do. I just tell them I'm at Marianne's and let them think we are reading magazines or whatever. This morning Dad asked, 'Are there boys there?' I replied, 'No, just Pete,' and that made him laugh. It was funny because he used to laugh all the time at things I'd say, and you'd hear him telling other people later. These days he doesn't listen to me much, just tells me what to do. He was in such a good mood that I stayed for an extra slice of toast and more tea, which is why I was there when the post arrived.

My godmother, who is also my Aunt Mary, sent me a belated (about two months late!) birthday card with some money in it. She used to send books, but they were always the kind that I would have read years before so I'm glad that she sends cash now. I really must make the effort to visit her soon.

I called Marianne and asked her did she want to come into town to do some clothes shopping. Club Havana is on again in a couple of days and it would be good to have a better time than the last time. They made me take Mikey in the pushchair, but I didn't mind because with Marianne there she could watch him while I tried outfits on.

Marianne had me try on some stuff that I never would have gone near on my own. I ended up buying this pale green dress that is a bit girlie, but in a really edgy kind of way. I'm not explaining it very well, but it's *really* cool and looks amazing on me. I had enough left to buy a silver bracelet (probably not real silver) with a love heart hanging from it. The green dress matches my eyes and makes them really stand out. It's the most conservative thing I own, but it's so film star and creative that I love it.

Marianne and I take the same size shoes and she has these really high ones that are actually easy to walk in and she's going to lend them to me.

I was secretly glad to have a day away from riding as I was getting really sore, and Marianne said that it's nice to remember that there's a whole other world that's waiting for her once the stables close.

No matter how great I feel, it always gets back to the thing about the stables closing. I must get a plan together. This time I won't tell Marianne so she can't get in trouble with Martin.

I haven't written to Hellie and Charlie in ages and I feel a bit guilty about that.

10 JULY

Bad to worse on the baby front, although I don't feel as crummy after talking to Marianne about it. Dad has asked me to spend this weekend helping him re-paint the crib for the new baby. I asked him where would we put it, and he said that he had been 'meaning to talk to me about that.' That phrase always spells trouble. My bedroom is bigger than Mikey's so they want me to move out of mine and into his, so that the two babies can be in the one room.

I had assumed it would go in Dad's office and then maybe he might go back to having a real job instead of all those schemes he comes up with. No such luck. Idiot me, thinking it might all be effortless and feel good.

Sometimes Dad has ideas like this and then forgets them, but I am really panicked about my room as it sounds like he and Mum discussed it. He said we might as well make the changeover this weekend while we're doing the painting.

I am not losing my bedroom this summer on top of everything else! I went and talked to Mum about it and she said that I could stay in my room until a couple of weeks before the baby arrives. She's going to break it to Dad who will be pretty pissed off that I got Mum to reverse his decision. He really hates that, but he never wants to worry Mum.

I hate this new baby already.

Martin hasn't been at the stables for the past two days, so today I found myself grooming Arab, who isn't so frisky once you get used to him. Can't wait for the dance, it's all Marianne and I talk about.

YES!

GREAT GREAT GREAT DANCE GREAT

12 JULY

Last night the dance was *great*. I went round to Marianne's and we got ready together and then Pete met us outside the club. I didn't ask where Martin was as I hoped he wouldn't be coming. The bouncer at the door wolf-whistled at me, which normally I hate, but tonight it made me feel good.

At first I was really pissed off as NONE of the Rat Pack were there. Pete went off with this girl he met at the last dance. Marianne and I danced with these two Spanish guys, mainly because the short guy from before was making a beeline for Marianne and we had to save her from that. Hers was tall, which by the smile on her face was more than enough. Mine was kind of OK, very Spanish and going back to Barcelona the next day so I figured it was safe enough to snog him. Besides, it would have been a waste of a great outfit if I hadn't! His name was Juan and he likes to play 'table a-tenniiiis', and was 'learning English very much'. I told him to shut up and dance and he liked that.

Today Pete said he'd call in, so the afternoon should go by faster. When he is there in the shop it's like it always was and it's hard to remember that it's all different in so many ways. Sometimes I even forget about the new baby.

13 JULY

OK, desperation is kicking in like a wild, crazy elephant and I have to do something *now*. Marianne was on the phone in bits because the latest home she thought she had found for Shine turns out not to be taking her.

Also, nice as Spanish Juan was, he's no Johnny Saunders, so I must do something *big* to get Johnny's attention.

Also, I got an e-mail from Charlie about how her Dad took her to be a guest on a taping of a TV comedy show. Stuff like that happens to her all the time.

At breakfast I asked Mum if her friend Sadie still

worked on *Good Morning, Good Morning*, our local TV show (on in the mornings, naturally). It's a really big show and they often get some celebrities coming in. I know Sadie because when she broke her ankle two years ago I would go round and walk her dog. I call her Crazy Sadie in my head because she is so loud and large and wears multi-coloured clothes that belong in a paint shop rather than on a person, let alone on a TV producer.

It's weird with people who knew you when you were little because they keep talking to you like you're still six.

I decided just to go up there and arrived just as she was passing the reception desk. She greeted me like I was some long-lost daughter and ushered me into the studio building. It wasn't as glamorous as I thought a television studio would be. It wasn't luxurious or anything and reminded me of the big furniture shop where we got the new sofa.

Crazy Sadie had not stopped talking and dropping files and papers since reception. Finally she said, 'Now, I suppose you're here because you want to meet Austin Page?'

My brain went funny, like I'd fallen down the rabbit hole. I'm not his biggest fan (I think Adie is), but I'd seen him in about seven films, usually playing the guy who overcame everything and got the girl. I would have been *INSANE* to say no.

I said no. I then quickly explained about the stables, but again Crazy Sadie was talking instead of listening properly.

'Well, let's get Austin Page to sign something and then you can auction it and use the money to save the donkeys.'

I started to explain that it wasn't about money, but I realised at that point that she was never going to get what it was about, or put me on the show to talk about it, so I smiled and said, 'What a great idea.'

Austin Page was getting his make-up done and was half-asleep, and stunning looking. A huge tattooed bodyguard was busy reading a woman's weekly magazine, so good job I wasn't a maniac. The star himself looked as if he had done this a dozen times since Monday.

Crazy Sadie introduced herself as the producer, not that he seemed to care. She then introduced me to him. 'This is Tammy, my friend's daughter and she'd love you to sign something to save the donkeys.'

'Horses, actually,' I mumbled as I shook his hand.

Suddenly it was like another person took over his body, and he almost jumped out of his chair.

'I'd love to help. I used to ride horses every day growing up on the ranch. Do you like to ride? What's up that they need saving?'

Then we got into this whole discussion and I told him about each of the horses and what they were like. Then came the best bit, he literally gave me the shirt off his back, a really worn denim shirt. And signed his name across the back and he asked his bodyguard to get his boots from the corner, which he handed to me.

'People are always sending me shoes and sneakers and stuff so why don't you take these too? Hopefully you might be able to sell them if you need to raise money for an attorney or for moving the horses to their new homes.'

The make-up lady had an instant camera and took a picture of him presenting me with the shirt and boots and then he signed the instant photo, this time writing, 'To Tammy the horse saver, from your friend Austin Page.'

I dropped the stuff home, even the sight of Dad bringing the cot down from the attic didn't get to me. I couldn't take the grin off my face, even though I hadn't actually managed to get on the show.

It's weird how you can just decide to do something and then just do it and things feel different.

After hiding the stuff at the back of my wardrobe, I headed over to the stables for a quick visit before starting in the shop. I decided not to tell Marianne, because then I'd have to explain why I'd originally gone.

Martin was outside, having brought the computer out into the courtyard.

'So you weren't at the club last night?' I smiled.

'I was,' he said without looking up.

Must have arrived when we were with the Spanish guys. Good thing he wasn't there earlier or we might have felt like we had to hang out with him.

'My sister's out with Grimsby Town.'

I joined her in the field and she thought that the reason I was so flushed and excited was Juan, so I let her think that.

She told me that her Spanish guy had wanted to walk her home, but Pete kept hanging around and said he promised Martin he'd get her home safe. So she was a bit pissed off that she didn't get to kiss the Spanish guy goodnight. Sounds like Martin left early or maybe he was walking some poor, unfortunate girl home.

We arranged to meet tomorrow at my place to talk about what we would do to save the horses. Less than a month to go, so it's getting critical.

As I got back t...
I saw a thi...
abo...

14 JULY

When I got to the stables this morning, Indian was already gone, they had taken him yesterday afternoon. Marianne said that the new owners live on the other side of the country. At least now the poor thing won't be left unloved like some old M&M at the bottom of a schoolbag, (the pony that is, Marianne has always been loved!)

The power-hose is kept coiled at the back of the long stable block, so I was headed there as I'd decided to finish off the cleaning of Indian's old stall while waiting for Marianne to take me out on Copper Girl.

...ound to the courtyard with the hose, ...n, wiry man by the office. He was quite tall, ...t Marianne's height, with wrinkled, tanned skin, pale grey eyes and a full head of grey-white hair, although he didn't look old enough for that colouring, he looked about my Dad's age. He darted off before I had a chance to say 'Hi.' As I know all the owners of the other horses by now, I figured (with my amazing brain!) that he must have been a spy sent by Mr Saunders. I mean, the way he was near the office and then nipped off like that ...

I dropped the hose (I hadn't turned the water on yet) and ran to the field where Marianne rode Grimsby Town straight over to me.

When I told her about the man, she suggested we let Martin know. I don't like approaching him, I'm never sure how he'll react, so I got her to do the talking.

He listened closely, seeming a little alarmed, and then smiled, saying, 'Marianne, remember the time you found an old party shoe on the street and told everyone it was Cinderella's slipper?'

'I was FIVE,' she protested.

'Well, "spies?" I'm just saying the old flair for the dramatic hasn't abandoned you!'

And he laughed and walked away. Well, that told us!

M&N

I was exasperated enough to do anything, even pay another visit to the tennis club. Maybe I could have a casual conversation with Johnny about the people who work for his Dad, I needn't even mention the stables. Sometimes I feel so frustrated that I just do anything because I have to do *something*, even if it doesn't make sense. I waited until later in the morning, knowing there was no way Johnny Saunders would be up at such an early hour during the holidays. I had to talk to him for my own sake and for the horses. It was like I couldn't *not* do it, like a foreign power had taken over my brain.

When I arrived at the tennis club they were all there in the main lounge, Adie, Doris, Johnny, Sean, Jeremy, the lot of them, looking as amazing as I wasn't. All two dozen of them were tanned and glowing, wearing white, and the girls had gold jewellery and diamond earrings. I don't usually like it when people look the same, but they looked so amazing that I felt a bit jealous. I was in jeans, a grubby t-shirt and old sneakers, with my hair tied back with a piece of string I had borrowed from Kitten's toy stash.

'You'll have to leave, Tammy,' Adie said before hello, 'We're having a meeting about our end-of-summer dance. It's members only.'

'So, have you joined yet? You might have to sell your house to afford it!' Johnny asked, and everyone else started laughing. I suddenly realised that the last time I was there he had been making fun of me by handing me the membership form.

'Will I get you another form?' Doris simpered, and they all laughed again.

I was now redder than a tomato with heat stroke, and when I tried to say something, nothing came out. I suddenly knew that Johnny never had any intention of helping me save the stables.

'How are your "interesting" friends doing? Dad and I have a really big laugh about them,' Johnny sneered. He turned to the rest of the group and said, 'Two kids with no business brains trying to run a horse-riding stables.'

'Well they had been doing that very nicely for three years until your Dad came along,' I finally blurted out, way louder than I, or anyone else, expected. 'And by the way, if you tell him about this little conversation I'll inform him and everyone in the neighbourhood about how you've been hanging out with me in my parents' shop every afternoon.'

Johnny is stuck-up enough that such a rumour would be social death to him, so I'm not worried about a repeat of the last time we spoke. There's no way he'd even be able to get those words out to his Dad.

'Have you?' demanded Adie.

'Have I what?' snapped Johnny.

'Been hanging out in her shop?' Doris asked.

'Of course not!' he said dismissively, but he still sounded annoyed.

The up side of being obsessed with him for so long, and having spent so long watching him after school, is that I know he is addicted to Carmel Cluster bars.

'Then I guess you won't be wanting any more free Carmel Cluster bars,' I said nonchalantly as I walked away, leaving Johnny gaping open-mouthed, and leaving the rest of them to their doubt. I blew him a kiss to add fuel to the fire.

As I walked back out the doors of the clubhouse, something clicked in my head, big time; I felt like I'd been eating rotten cabbage for the last year, thinking it was caviar. Suddenly that perfect white smile looked like the fake grin of a cheap car salesman and I saw how lazy he was, being given everything, earning nothing. In two minutes I went from the point where I'd have walked over broken glass to be with him, to the point of wanting to feed it to him. What a loser!

I found the poem I had written about Johnny, tore

it up and wrote a new one. This one doesn't rhyme because the words 'idiot,' 'asshole,' and 'complete bastard' sound great already. I found that raffle ticket he had handed me at the New Year's dance (now realising he meant it as an insult like I couldn't buy my own) and tore it into pieces and flushed it symbolically down the toilet. I wished it was his head.

OK, I will now come up with a plan to make Johnny Saunders sorry he even met me, AND save the stables. It's war, and it's personal!!

15 JULY

Rather than going to the stables this morning I went around to Pete's to borrow his old camera.

'Pete, it's a stupid camera, not your firstborn, you'll get it back tonight,' I implored.

He insisted on coming with me, which was actually a good idea as Pete is completely nuts and would do anything. I told him the plan was go to the Saunders' house, to find the man I saw, take a picture of him, then hang out at the stables and take a picture of him there also. The other part of the plan was to find anything that we might be able to use to get Mr Saunders to back off or anything that might embarrass Johnny.

'Like a clipped coupon?' Pete joked, and for the first time I joined in, adding, 'Or a pair of supermarket-bought trainers.'

I can now understand why he has never liked the Rat Pack.

'So, Tammy. Why do you think Marianne won't go out with me?' Pete surprised me with this question halfway to Johnny's place.

'That would be the brain thing,' I replied, 'As in, she has one.'

'No, really,' he said. And then it hit me, Pete, who has never been serious about a girl in all the years I knew him, had it bad for Marianne! I got a sudden rush of excitement, but played it cool because I'd *sooooo* love them to get together.

I explained that a girl doesn't want to feel like the prized turkey on a turkey farm, she wants to feel like the sole dove in the cote.

'Huh?'

Metaphors were never Pete's thing.

'Stop chatting-up, dancing with, dating and mentioning other girls.'

'Check!'

'*All* other girls.'

'For real?'

'For real.'

'And when you talk to Marianne, don't joke around all the time, ask her some real questions about her life, and give a few sensible answers when she asks you stuff.'

'I was thinking I could just wow her with my new dance move, the horseshoe shuffle,' and he started to do this dance that was a cross between disco, hip-hop and a gallop.

'Pete! That's exactly the kind of thing you need to NOT do.'

'Gotcha.'

'Also, stay away from her for a while; when she teaches you to ride every day, she'll be too used to you, she won't have time to miss you.'

'Are all girls this conniving?'

'It's called wisdom, little man.'

Johnny's house is huge, we saw the swimming pool and basketball court from the gate.

I explained again that we were looking for evidence of anything that could help. Granted, it was a pretty broad brief.

'You take the back, I'll take the front,' Pete said in a bad James Bond impression.

And before I knew it I was sneaking around the back of the house, camera in shaking hand, while

Pete chatted to the housekeeper on the doorstep. From where I was I could hear him pretending to apply for a job as a gardener.

I suddenly realised how mental this idea was, but the sight of a tennis racket abandoned by the pool got me angry enough to carry on. I still can't believe I did this! There was no sign of anyone around. The French sliding doors at the back were open, so I slipped in. Through the conservatory was a living room and an office to the side, and I decided this would be my best bet. I sneaked into the office, my heart beating louder and faster than Arab's hooves full-gallop on dry grass. The large mahogany desk was a mess of papers. I knew I wouldn't have time to read them all, so I just snapped a dozen or so close-up pictures and legged it back out the sliding doors. I got around to the front of the house again just in time to see the housekeeper shutting the door in Pete's face as he said, 'Petunias! You'll find I'm the local expert in petunias.'

We ran back up the road and didn't stop running and laughing until we got to Pete's place. There's probably nothing in the pictures, but at least I now feel like it's possible to fight back.

19 JULY

I haven't written in this for the past three days, for reasons that will become obvious, but I want to write it all down because I will always want to remember.

After the last time I wrote, I woke to what sounded like Pete on the balcony, knocking at my bedroom window. According to my alarm clock it was just after two a.m., so I was going to ignore him, but the knocking sounded more urgent than usual and I saw a bunch of voicemails had been left on my phone, and I suddenly thought he might have found something in the photos. It was raining really hard so I whispered through the curtain and glass just loud enough to be heard over the rain, 'Don't think you're coming in here all wet.'

'I don't need to come in, I just need to talk,' said a voice that wasn't Pete's. I pulled back the curtain and saw Martin, sitting on the large branch of the tree with one hand on the trunk and the other on the balcony. He was completely soaking wet, his hair plastered to the side of his face. He was only wearing a thin sweater and jeans, no jacket or anything. I felt really confused.

'What's wrong?' I asked, afraid something had happened to the horses.

'I need your help,' he said.

I couldn't believe it, I had never heard him ask anyone for help, not with the tiniest little thing. I found that I didn't have the heart to hate him right then, he looked so desperate.

'Hold on,' I said. I closed the curtain and went to put on a sweater and jeans of my own over my t-shirt and shorts. I looked out onto the landing and saw that the lights were off in Dad's office and in Mum and Dad's bedroom. Going back to open my window to let Martin in, part of my brain was screaming that I was an idiot, I'd be caught for certain, but I went ahead anyway.

I put a towel down on my bed and he sat there, dripping. Stupidly enough I was thinking how glad I was that the room was so tidy and that I had so many books out on view. He took it all in as he caught his breath and dried his hair with another towel, which I'd handed him. I was glad that the desk no longer had 'I LOVE JOHNNY SAUNDERS' notices all over it like it did last week.

I sat cross-legged on the other end of the bed and listened as he shivered from the wet clothes and explained what was going on.

'You know that man you said you saw at the stables?' Martin started, 'Well, he does exist, his name is Sam and I've known him for the last month, although Dad knew him all his life. I had to pretend otherwise so that no-one would guess about this business deal I have going with him, a deal that might allow him to work the stables. He knows a lot about horses from all over the place, he's like the guardian of all horses. He called me late this evening, not about our business venture, but about a pony that needs to be rescued. I've been out to see the pony, and it's bad. The problem is that there are some people who think it should be theirs, and want to sell it to the pet-food factory once it's dead.'

'So you have to steal it?' I asked, amazed that this was all happening.

'Not really steal it, as it doesn't belong to the other

people who want it, and the real owners just abandoned it. Bottom line is, I need help and I need it now, tonight. Marianne has to be at home so she can make sure that Gran doesn't notice I'm gone. She suggested I ask Pete to come with me, but I think you'd be better. I called Pete and he told me about the best way to get hold of you at this hour, the tree and all that.'

I threw him my large grey sweater that reaches my knees and looked away while he changed into it, leaving his own damp one on the end of the bed.

'Why me?' I was utterly bewildered.

'Because you have a real feeling for things, for horses.' With that, he jumped up quickly and said, 'So, are you up for it?'

And that's how I found myself wearing my Dad's old mac in the pouring rain at two in the morning, being helped out of my own back-garden tree. We ran in silence to the main road and jumped on the cross-town night bus just as it was about to pull away from the stop. Martin already had our bus fares to hand, which made me smile.

It was a bit embarrassing at first, sitting opposite each other at the back of the bus, and I wished I'd taken a second to brush my hair. Finally my curiosity got the better of me and I broke the silence.

'Martin? I'm a bit confused. Why go to all the trouble to save this horse when you have nine others that need new homes?'

He took a moment and looked serious before answering.

'Because it's what my Mum and Dad used to do. If ever there was a sick or unwanted horse or pony they would take it in. That's how we got Copper Girl, Arab and Grimsby Town. Last year Marianne and I stayed awake all night when Shine arrived all starving and beaten, looking after her, willing her to live. We heard about her through a friend of Sam – Sam's the man we are going to meet now. When I can help a horse in any way I think … I just feel like Mum and Dad are not really gone, that somehow they are still here with us, that any minute now Dad will walk in with a bucket of bran mash or a horse blanket.'

He half-smiled and I felt that I would follow him to the ends of the earth to help save a pony. I was glad I had grabbed Dad's other old mac for him and he was no longer shivering.

Sam was surprised to see me there to say the least, and his light grey eyes smiled, even if his mouth was set. Martin reassured him that I was there to help and could be trusted. Sam already had the sick animal in a horsebox, parked on the edge of a petrol station forecourt. The neighbourhood looked rough and I hoped we'd be out of there soon.

Inside the horsebox was a thin and straggly looking brown pony, smaller than Copper Girl, with a white mark on her nose. Sam told me her name was Feather, on account of the white mark looking like a feather. She was lying on her side and was breathing in short, panting breaths like I'd seen Arab do after jumping. Martin and I got in the back with Feather while Sam drove, and during the journey Martin rubbed her down with handfuls of hay while I stroked her head gently and kept my eyes closed to combat the motion sickness I was starting to feel.

When we finally got to the stables, I couldn't believe they were going to move her, but Sam explained that a friend of his had lent them the horsebox without real permission and they needed to get it back down to the countryside immediately. So we coaxed Feather to stand and moved her to the spare stable at the very end.

Sam nodded goodbye and sped off on his seven-hour trip to return the horsebox. It was raining even harder now as Martin left to go and fetch the vet. He'd wanted to make sure that Feather actually arrived safely before getting the vet out of bed. He asked me if I'd be OK on my own and I smiled bravely and said I wouldn't be alone, the horses would be with me. I wished Marianne hadn't brought Kitten home.

The next hour was one of the longest I've ever known. Sitting there in the semi-darkness in the middle of the night, without Martin, with Feather sweating and lying restlessly. I remembered the time I was seven and had the mumps, and how Dad stayed up dabbing my forehead with a cold cloth while Mum drove over to the all-night pharmacy to get me the medicine the doctor had just prescribed. I wondered if my Dad had felt as lonely and scared as I did right then. The rain made me feel even more alone.

Eventually, I began to sing to poor little Feather, probably as much to comfort myself as her. I sang 'Yellow Bird', as it was the one Mum and Dad would sing to me as a baby, and now we sing it to Mikey all the time,

'Yellow Bird, high up in banana tree, yellow bird you sit all alone like me.
Did your lady friend leave the nest again? That is very bad, makes me feel so sad,
you can fly away in the sky-away,
you more lucky than me.'

It was either the sound of my singing or the sound of the rain that allowed Martin to stand in the stable doorway unnoticed. Only when the vet slammed his car door in the lane did I see Martin standing there. There was no time to wonder how long he'd been listening as it was all action stations, the vet having us both fetch things for him. Martin had left his mac behind in the stable and was soaking wet once more.

The vet was a kind man and gave Feather an injection to help with her pain and left saying that Feather had been through a lot and that the night would tell.

We had set up a small electric fire so the stable began to feel cosier. Martin had taken off his dripping-wet sweater, and his boots and socks, and moved about with his t-shirt and jeans sticking to him, but getting less damp all the time. I had managed to stay pretty dry and hung Dad's macs on the on the nail at the door.

Martin looked so strong and certain that I suddenly felt it would all turn out fine. As I watched him re-read the instructions from the vet I realised that what I had taken for sulkiness in the past was in fact his intense concentration, his absolute focus on whatever was in front of him or in his head. I wanted to say sorry for not being nicer before, but I couldn't get the words out, so instead I ran to the office with one of the macs over my head, and brought him back a hot mug of tea. Also, I had cleverly brought some energy bars from the kitchen at home when I was fetching the macs from downstairs. He looked surprised and grateful for the tea and the bars, which he ate four of.

I knew I should get home in a couple of hours because I was needed to mind Mikey while Mum and Dad went for a doctor's appointment about the new baby, but I also knew I had to stay right there with Martin and the pony.

We sat side by side looking at Feather, with me asking the odd question about the time they had nursed Copper Girl.

Suddenly, Feather began to breathe with even greater difficulty and Martin got down on his knees, stroking her head and whispering something in her ear. I could see his eyes had welled up with tears and he had completely forgotten anyone else was there. I suddenly realised what he already knew, that Feather might be dying. For an hour he stayed like that, whispering and stroking. A single tear fell onto Feather's face. I sat still in the corner on the hay, my arms wrapped around my legs, completely quiet. I felt empty, like we all might as well be dying too.

The next thing I knew I was waking up as the sun shone on my face through the open stable door, from high in the sky. I was lying in the same bundle of hay, with a clean horse blanket over me and Martin's (now dry) sweater making a pillow under my face. I sat up slowly, happy that Feather was still there, but then I noticed that she was completely covered with horse blankets, even her head. Martin was sitting on the upturned bucket now, obviously waiting for me to wake.

'She died an hour ago,' he said, gently.

'I'm so sorry,' I said.

I wanted to go over and hug him, but instead we just sat looking at each other. At that moment Marianne and Mrs Miggs arrived.

There was something really comforting about having an adult there, although it was weird to see her at the stables, but not as weird as when Adie and Doris were there.

Marianne hugged me, and I thought for a moment I was going to cry. But I knew that it was even tougher for her and Martin, that they would be thinking about their parents, so I forced myself not to.

I should have called home, but I figured any

damage would already be done and I couldn't stand to break away from where I was. I wanted to think of something to say to Martin, to let him know that he did all he could, but I couldn't speak. I didn't know what to do or what to say, so I numbly helped Marianne feed and water the other horses, while Martin and Mrs Miggs made some calls from the office. We had a late breakfast in their house, a quiet breakfast, and then I had to face going back to what I knew would be a huge storm at home. Just as I left Martin grabbed my hand and squeezed it, looking away as he did so.

Only when I got to the front door did I look at my watch. It was two in the afternoon. Mum and Dad were waiting in the kitchen when I got in and I could tell they'd been angry for ages. Mum put her hand on Dad's sleeve to quiet him.

'Tammy, sweetheart,' she started. 'We had a doctor's appointment this morning, remember? And you didn't leave a note, we were worried.'

But Dad just cut through, shouting about how they didn't know if I'd been attacked or when I was coming back and how selfish I was .... He yelled and ranted at me until I just burst out crying. I was sobbing so hard that I thought my body would break. I just couldn't keep any of it in anymore, and I fell to the floor and cried for everything, everything that I couldn't make right.

Dad stopped yelling then, and put his arms around me nervously and hugged me before lifting me up like he used to when I was little and carrying me to the sofa.

He kept saying, 'I'm sorry Tam, it's OK, it's OK, we'll sort it all out.' He pulled Mikey's large play-rug over me and I cried some more and then I must have fallen asleep again.

When I woke up again Dr Benson was standing over me.

'I'm not sick,' I told him, 'Just sad'.

Mum and Dad were sitting in the armchairs opposite.

'How about you tell us everything?' Mum said.

'We can only help when we know exactly what is going on,' added Dr Benson.

I was too tired to fight or pretend any more, and stared into the fireplace as I let them know everything that was on my mind and in my heart.

I told them how I felt pressured to do well at school, how I felt trapped by having to work in the shop every afternoon, how I felt that they expected me to mind Mikey whenever they wanted and how I figured it would all get much worse once the new baby came. I also said that I missed Mum since Gran died, that she seemed to be so down and distracted since then, and that I missed Dad talking to me and having fun, that I felt they didn't love me any more.

Dr Benson then said, 'I hear you are hanging out with new friends, are they getting you to drink or take drugs at all?'

Typical! As soon as a teenager gets upset at how adults are treating them, the adults need to think it's something else. I had to laugh at that one, and explained that Marianne and Martin had been teaching me to ride and care for horses, and that they are the smartest, healthiest, hardest-working people I know. I then kept talking and told them all about the problems with the stables, but I left out the bit about breaking into the Saunders' house.

I finally looked over at Dad who was staring at the carpet, looking really sad.

Mum gave me a kiss and told me to go up to bed and rest, and I guess they stayed there talking about me. It felt good to not be holding it all inside anymore, but I'm also a bit scared about what they'll do next.

I've been in bed now for a day and a half, with Mum bringing me food. I've told her I'm not ready to talk again yet. I've just been gazing at the ceiling and writing this.

I keep wondering what Martin and Marianne are thinking about me not being around, I just can't get it together to talk to anyone.

I'm feeling tired again, I think I'll sleep some more.

VISITORS!!

20 JULY

'Visitors!' Dad announced brightly so as to let me know he was cool with it, and Pete, Martin and Marianne traipsed into my room. Luckily I had finally showered and put on my best pyjamas earlier in the day. I had even remembered to brush my hair for once!

The guys teased me about finally letting them in the conventional way, through a door, and we had to explain to Marianne about the wall and the tree and all that. Pete sat on the floor, Martin on the chair and Marianne on the bed.

We took our time going over the story from everyone's point of view. I knew there were things I wasn't saying and I wondered if it was the same with the others. Marianne said that their parents' car crash had happened on a rainy night so she had been completely panicked when Martin and I didn't show up by mid-morning and neither of our phones was working. She didn't want to leave the house in case we came back there and she was too afraid to go and look at the stables in case we weren't there. That was why she went and told her granny about the call from Sam and trying to rescue Feather. She found that once she started, Mrs Miggs had a way of asking questions that made her tell everything about how we are all trying to save the stables. Apparently their gran called my parents later that day and we are all having a big meeting in her dining room, as soon as I'm up and about, to sort out the entire situation.

Martin told the story from his point of view telling how he tried to save Feather while I slept; I wished so much I had stayed awake, but he said he was glad I was asleep because it was heartbreaking to watch Feather's breathing get so laboured. After we talked about all that (I just said Mum and Dad were angry about me being out, but they got over it) we started to focus on how to save the stables, determined now to be able to help other horses even though we couldn't save poor little Feather.

Martin is confident that we can find a way to save the stables. He and Sam have been setting up an internet business selling horse merchandise such as mugs, books, posters and all that. They have worked out that if things keep going as well as they have been it will make enough money to pay Sam a real salary so he can run the stables. Then Sam can give lessons too and make more money from that.

They stayed for about three hours and it was so much fun. Pete then got up to leave to finish a project. He winked at me when he said that, and I knew it meant he was working on the photographs that I'd taken in Mr Saunders' home-office. Marianne then said she had to pick up some supplies for the meeting, which would have left just Martin and me in the room, but he quickly mumbled something about letting me get some rest and headed for the door as his sister made her way downstairs. As I put my head back down on the pillow he turned in the doorway and said, 'Thanks Tammy, I don't know what I'd do without you.' He then walked back across the room took up my right hand and kissed it, before almost running out and down the stairs!!!

I didn't have time to think about that too much as Mum and Dad then came upstairs. They said they were sorry, that they had been taking me for granted and that they are really proud to have such a caring and hard-working daughter. Apparently Dad spent last night on the phone until he found a local woman who'll work in the shop full-time so Mum can look after Mikey and the new baby.

He told me that his businesses have started to make money so that we will be able to start taking holidays again from next year, and we'll have more money for clothes and classes and things like that. I suddenly realised that it had been difficult for him to pay for my dance classes last year, and I gave them both a big hug and told them I *like* helping out, just not *all* the time. We are going to arrange things so that everyone gets to pull their weight and get whatever else they need.

I also told them that I don't want to be a doctor, I want to be a vet, and they said that whatever I decide to be, they are behind me.

I can't really describe how I feel right now, it's as if everything was all at angles and now it's just clicked into place. I feel pretty confident about saving the stables now that the adults are on board.

YAWN

PAPERWORK

WHAT IF....?

22 JULY

Sam, Mrs Miggs, my mum and dad, Pete's mum, and me, Martin, Marianne and Pete all sat around Mrs Miggs's big dining room table. Mrs Miggs had made coffee as well as tea for the occasion, and Marianne had bought about three packets of cookies for each person, which gave us a good laugh. We got started as soon as the vet and Mrs Miggs's lawyer arrived.

There was quite a lot of boring stuff about legal things and I know that Marianne and Pete were trying as hard as I was not to yawn. I don't quite know how, but it is all getting sorted, and all they need to do is to send some stuff to the local authorities.

YA

As we were all leaving the meeting Martin signalled to Pete and me to meet them at the stables at eight that night.

We were kind of relieved that the stables are saved, but not completely elated about it.

Marianne said what we were all feeling, 'It's not enough. We need to make sure Saunders leaves us alone for good, we need to really show him that he doesn't have power over us.'

Pete opened the envelope he'd been holding. He had finally got to use the equipment for enlarging the photos.

I quickly explained to a shocked Martin and Marianne what Pete and I had done last week. They couldn't believe it, and Martin wanted to look stern, but kept laughing with each new twist.

We eventually calmed down and looked at the pictures of the documents. All of the papers were regular invoices and accounts, except one, a handwritten page that we didn't really understand.

Marianne read it aloud, there was a lot of language about offshore accounts, creative accounting, moving funds through buying foreign currency, nothing that really made sense to me. Martin grabbed the photo and read it again, silently.

'It means we've got Saunders,' he grinned. 'This is

a note to his bookkeeper about hiding money from a deal so he doesn't have to pay taxes on it. It's completely illegal. And it's written in his own handwriting and signed with his initials.

'Should we tell Gran and Sam right now?' Marianne suggested.

'No!' the rest of us said together.

'We need to pay him a visit,' Martin decided, 'Sam says Saunders is hoping to run for local government next year, he'll want this kept under wraps.'

We decided all four of us would go, no one wanted to miss this. We arranged to meet at seven in the morning outside Pete's place, which is the closest to the Saunders' house. That way we can surprise him, and maybe Johnny, at breakfast.

23 JULY

out for a walk with pete,
marianne & martin. back
before 10 a.m. or will phone.

I woke up early enough to look great and leave a detailed note for Mum and Dad,

'Out for a walk with Pete, Marianne and Martin. Back before 10 a.m. or will phone.'

Everyone was ten minutes early. None of us spoke a word as we walked up the road to the Saunders' house and stood in front of those huge gates.

As we stared at the house, Martin broke the silence saying, 'One day I'll own a house like this, with enough land behind it to breed and rescue hundreds of horses.'

'The difference is, you'd appreciate it,' I said, and then wished I hadn't, as it was a bit personal and I thought I might be about to blush. To cover it, I walked up to the front door and pressed the bell. After a couple of minutes the housekeeper answered, took one look at Pete and said they still didn't need a gardener. Martin put his foot in the doorway, and said we were there to see Mr Saunders.

'About the election,' he added.

She reluctantly let us all in and asked us to wait in the hallway, but we were way too wired for waiting so we hustled past her and into the kitchen where we could see Mr Saunders sitting at the breakfast bar, eating toast. When he saw us he thought we must be there to see Johnny and sent the housekeeper upstairs to wake him.

'Actually, we've come to see you,' Pete said, waving the enlarged photo in front of him.

Saunders didn't even glance at it, he just smiled this really condescending smile, which was exactly like the one Miss Reagan gives when we can't answer a simple maths question.

He stood up and started to wag his finger at us, as if we were naughty puppies.

'Look, this is business. You are too young to run a horse-riding stable and I need that land for a new building venture. I was just going around to your grandmother's house today to make her a very generous offer.'

I told him that the only generous offer he could make would be to offer to move to a small island far away and leave us alone forever.

'Fiery little thing, aren't you?' he sneered, and I was just about to give him a real earful when Johnny stepped into the room and asked us what we were doing there.

Martin took charge.

'We have come here to explain to your father that our horse business is now being run by an outside corporation, the land is not for sale and never will be, and that if he doesn't keep away from us in the future we will be talking to the papers,' he said.

Johnny laughed in that same dismissive way as his father and said, 'Tell them Dad, how all the editors are friends of yours.'

'Well, we'll see what great friends they are once they realise the size of the scandal,' Martin smiled.

I took complete joy in pointing to the photo in Pete's hand and saying, 'We have evidence about your Dad's illegal financial dealings. My parents might not be as rich as yours, but we earn our money honestly.'

Mr Saunders went ballistic at that point, grabbed the photo, saw what it was and set fire to it in the kitchen sink.

Pete laughed and I knew he was trying really hard not to do his best Sherlock Holmes voice as he said, 'I have ten copies made, all in envelopes with different people, ready to get sent to the papers and TV stations as soon as I give the word.'

Johnny noticed his dad was now getting dangerously angry and started to plead pathetically with Pete, and then turned to me and said, 'Tammy, come on, we're friends aren't we?'

'No,' I said, 'I have much higher standards for friendship. My friends don't make me look small in front of others or walk away from me as soon as other people walk into the room, my friends get that I'm a good person. These are my friends.'

'So,' Pete said, 'Let's just agree to stay away from each other.'

Martin led the way and we left the house, knowing that would be way stronger than getting thrown out. Neither Johnny nor Mr Saunders said a thing. They knew we had them.

1 AUGUST

I haven't been writing in this for the last week or so because I've been helping Mum sort through Mikey's old stuff in the evenings to see what to keep for the new baby. Some of the stuff was mine when I was born, which is amazing to think of.

We also moved me into the smaller room, but the way Dad painted the furniture and the walls looks so amazing that it actually feels bigger. They've also given me the space under the stairs, which is big enough for me to stand in, and although it's just wide enough to fit a desk and chair I've left those in my room. Instead I've made a den out of it by putting in some carpet that was in the attic, and I'm busy making a dozen cushions from all the stuff in the old dress-up box, which I'll scatter around for lying and sitting on. I have two shelves in my new little den, one with next year's schoolbooks and one with some new novels that I want to read over the next couple of months. I'm not telling anyone else apart from Marianne about this place, as I love to just shut myself away with a bowl of cereal, my music playing, and a book or this journal. I'm here right now and realise that I need to get a lamp as the light in here is about what you'd get from striking a match.

The only downside to moving rooms is that now there's no way I can get any visitors in the middle of the night!

I've been at the stables every morning and Pete and Marianne seem to be getting on quite nicely, and having real conversations! Pete listened to my advice about not crowding her and is at the stables every second day, so I get my time with her on those mornings and my time with Pete when he drops into the shop. I'm helping with training in the new woman in the afternoons. None of us have really been talking about what happened in the past few weeks, it's as if we've had enough drama for now and want to have things as normal as possible.

Martin hasn't been around at all for the last week.

He's off with Sam at trade fairs for their business. I have loads of stories to tell him about how good I'm getting on Copper Girl, I even cantered today for about ten seconds. It was amazing, not nearly as bouncy as trotting. I think he's back tomorrow.

Every night as I fall asleep I think about that rainy night with Feather. I can't believe I was so wrong about Martin and how convinced I was that I was right.

2 AUGUST

I am *really* confused right now. I thought Martin would be back today, but it turns out he's not back until tomorrow evening so I won't even get to see him until the day after that. That's not the weird bit, the weird bit is that I was *so* disappointed, more than I used to be if Johnny wasn't at a dance. I think, no in fact I *know,* that I've somehow fallen for Martin. Somehow between yelling at him and crying and sitting up all night with a pony, I fell for him. There, I said it. I hope it doesn't last because he is great but still impossible, I mean he's Marianne's *brother* and anyway I don't even know if he has a girlfriend or anything. He must have seen me with the Spanish guy and maybe thinks I'm going out with him. I guess it was only a matter of time before I managed to make things complicated again!

In the shop I have spent a lot of time running back through the last few weeks, but now I find I'm also daydreaming about him, imagining things that might happen. Like thinking how it would feel if he danced with me at Club Havana, or how it might be if he asked me to go to a film with him. I hope he doesn't find out as I know he thinks of me just as his sister's little friend who is a bit mentally unhinged. I'd *die* if anyone knew, especially him. I wonder if Marianne ever told him about the crush I had on Johnny for all that time. He must think I am *SO* stupid!! And I'd have to agree.

It's a pity there are no more dances at Club Havana until Halloween, otherwise I could go there and try to get fixated on someone else.

Marianne and I don't talk about the Rat Pack at all any more and I don't think about them either.

I was the first to arrive this morning and couldn't believe what I saw. It took me a full minute to take it all in. Someone had wrecked the place, put saddles and bridles all over the ground, spray painted the stables with horrible things, pictures and words like 'die scum', and worse. I quickly checked each of the horses and they seemed fine so I ran over to Marianne's and got there just as she was leaving. We called Pete and raced back to survey the damage.

'Right,' she said, sounding like her brother. 'Sam and Martin don't need to come back to this. Pete, get some white spirits and bleach, Tammy, get some cloths and newspaper. I'll get the tack back inside.'

We were so amazed at Marianne being so efficient that we just went off and did as she asked. I explained to Mum what had happened and she said I needn't work in the shop that afternoon.

However, it was obvious after the first hour of scrubbing that there was no way we would get it done before Martin and Sam got back. We knew they would pitch-in, but we really wanted for them not to have to deal with it after working so hard at the trade fairs. There were still nine more stables covered in red and blue spray paint! It was coming off, but it was hard work.

'Who would do such a thing?' asked Marianne, 'Mr Saunders would be too scared to, but who would be *stupid* enough?'

'Johnny!' Pete and I said together.

Just at that moment, I found a gold bracelet lying in a tiny pile of hay. It hadn't been there the day before as I remembered sweeping that area. I felt sick as I looked at it and saw the initials D-A-Y, Doris was really proud of her initials spelling 'DAY', kind of like the 1950s actress Doris Day.

I told the others I had to run home, but instead I went round to the tennis club. I wasn't so much angry as determined. I felt like I had to close them down and put a stop to the way they'd been treating me so badly all these years. It took them hurting my friends to make me strong enough to do something. It was now barely nine a.m., but already Doris and Johnny and a few others were sitting round the clubhouse. Johnny was laughing, but he stopped as soon as I arrived, he looked scared, and rightly so.

I didn't wait for anyone to insult me this time, instead I threw the bracelet at Doris and said in a loud enough voice that everyone (adults and kids alike) could hear, that she left it behind when she and Johnny vandalised the stables. I then said that we would have the place back in shape by sundown and if they ever came within a mile of us again, I'd call the police. Doris started to go, 'I... I... I... ', but couldn't get a sentence out.

Jeremy stepped over to me and said that I couldn't go around making accusations like that, and I asked him if he's ever seen Johnny up this early during the holidays. I then said that at the stables we have surveillance cameras that caught everything, and that I was happy to come down here and screen it for everyone, (not true but they didn't know that). Johnny and Doris were looking grey and nervous and twitchy.

'Go ahead, deny it!' I offered.

They said nothing, which was proof enough for

everyone. They all just looked at me.

I couldn't stand to be around them a moment longer so I just walked out and back to the stables, bringing food with me that Mum let me take from the shop. For the next two hours we worked away and were just about to stop for something to eat and some mugs of tea when the most *amazing* thing happened. Up the lane we could hear voices and footsteps, and suddenly about twenty teenagers appeared in the courtyard, including Jeremy (but no sign of Adie). Sean, another Rat Pack guy stepped forward and said that they believed us that Doris and Johnny had done it, that they had been plotting something for days. Jane, a girl I knew from dancing, said that they were all there to help. Sure enough, they had changed out of their tennis whites.

Marianne had everyone hard at work scrubbing away within minutes, and by dinnertime the stables looked more amazing than they had ever done. It felt really good to have all those new people around. We got to know them better during the afternoon and they really are pretty cool. Some of them came over and apologised for the way they had acted when I came in during their dance meeting. They even invited me to play there as their guest any time I wanted and said that they could lend me anything I needed! I guess I was wrong about them too, but by now I'm used to being wrong about people.

The look on Martin's face as he got out of Sam's car was priceless, there were so many people and the stable-walls were shining. Marianne and I were falling over ourselves trying to tell him what happened and eventually he made sense of what we were saying as he took in how great the place was looking. We stayed there until six and all the others had gone home to eat.

Pete and I went back with Marianne and Martin, and Mrs Miggs made the most amazing dinner of shepherd's pie and chocolate mousse cake. She waited until we were all finished eating before telling us that my mother and Crazy Sadie (except she called her Sadie the TV producer) had phoned. Apparently Sadie wants us on the show tomorrow to talk about the stables and the way some people treat horses and to report on what happened with the vandalising this morning! Mum had called the station right after I left with the cloths.

I am now too excited to sleep and have tried on five outfits already. Mum says my new green dress, but she just wants me to look 'normal!'

4 AUGUST

I *did* wear the green dress to the studio and when Martin saw me in it he whistled through his teeth and said, 'Hey, your green dress. I hope this doesn't mean you'll be kissing any Spanish blokes. I don't think I could stand it a second time.'

I nearly fell over, I was that surprised, and Marianne even raised an eyebrow at me.

Pete decided he didn't want to be on the show, that he was more of a behind the camera person, which is funny when you consider all the effort he usually puts into being the centre of attention. We had a good laugh when we had to get make-up put on, even Martin had to wear some foundation so as not to look too pale under the studio lights. Only then did I remember the last time I was there and thought I must tell the others about meeting Austin Page and getting the signed stuff.

We were walked out onto the set and the sound girl hooked up microphones to us. We had to sit there while the news anchor read the news and weather and then it was our turn. As soon as it started my nerves left me.

First the host asked Marianne about the stables, then asked me about how some people abuse horses and how we at the stables rescue them, and finally Martin talked about the on-line shop for horse stuff. She then asked me was it true that the film star Austin Page had autographed one of his shirts and given me his boots to raise money for the horses.

I was floored by the question as I wasn't expecting it and hadn't told anyone (Crazy Sadie must have told the host), but managed to blurt out, 'Yes, and we'll be auctioning them this week to raise money for ... em .... for the Feather Fund to save abused horses.'

Martin quickly said, 'The details will be on the website later today.'

It was all over in less than fifteen minutes and I think we did really well. The others pounced on me as soon as we were back out in the car park.

'Austin Page!!!!' was all Marianne could say, over and over.

'Tammy, you never told us, and you're supposed to be our best friend!' Pete said in mock offence, 'Or are you going to be hanging out with Austin all the time now?'

'Well,' I teased him, 'I'll need someone to hang out with now that you're with Marianne all the time.'

They both pretended to hit me. I am *so* sure there is something going on there. I told them what had happened the last time I came to the studio and about the shirt and boots that were at my house, and the photo to prove they are authentic.

We went up to the stables where six of the tennis club crowd were waiting. They explained that they are good with horses so they helped us with exercising the horses whose owners are away, and with the grooming.

Martin rode Arab and then disappeared off to put the Austin Page stuff up on the website. I can't believe how much I used to take it for granted when he had time to teach me to ride. In only three more weeks we'll be back at school and I wonder if I'll get to see him at all after that?

6 AUGUST

A really funny thing happened this afternoon. Adie came into the shop, and asked me if I had a moment. She said she had nothing to do with what Johnny and Doris did. I said that I knew that. Then I took all my courage in my hands and said, 'How could you hang out with Doris? She's so mean.'

'I know,' she said. I always wanted for us to be friends again, but Doris would give me such a hard time if I said anything nice about you, that I thought I was stuck. I'm not hanging out with her anymore, and I don't blame you if you never want to speak to me again.'

'Not my style,' I grinned.

She looked so miserable that I said, 'Hey, I know you're the biggest Austin Page fan in the world. Would you like me to tell you about him?' As we chatted it was as if the years rolled back and things were like before. I know she won't be my best friend like Marianne, Charlie and Hellie, but at least things won't be so awkward now.

I showed her the picture of me and Austin and she looked like she was going to pass out. She then offered me a swap, and I had to get her to say it again. She was offering me the old horsebox she had bought when she got Indian in exchange for the boots and shirt. When I didn't accept right away she started to explain how it was one that you drove, not just a trailer, and how it took two horses and a whole bunch of other stuff.

'But won't your parents mind? I mean those things cost a fortune.'

'They won't even notice it gone,' she said. 'They just sort of throw money at me so they don't have to be real parents.' Suddenly I realised that she hung out with the tennis club crowd because she felt bad and insecure. Still, I didn't want to make the trade right away so I told her she'd have to ask Martin, and then quickly changed it to say that I'd try and convince Martin. That way I had a reason to go and find him.

Then, she amazed me as she walked out of the shop. She said, 'It doesn't even matter about the Austin Page stuff, I want you guys to have the horsebox, you deserve it.'

I do want her to have the Austin stuff, but it was cool that she said that.

Martin was closing up by the time I got there just before nine, and I suddenly felt ashamed remembering the last time I had gone looking for him at this hour and ended up yelling at him. We sat on the wall in the half-light and I told him about Adie's suggestion and he just sat there and stared at me while I explained it again, certain I'd been unclear the first time.

'Tammy?'

I wondered what was coming next.

'Does magic always follow you around this way?'

And then he scooped me off the wall and swung me around, both of us laughing. I was sure he was about to kiss me when Pete and Marianne came out of one of the stables to see what all the noise was about.

They had news for me too. Apparently the tennis club dance committee are not allowed to have the end of summer dance in the clubhouse this year because someone pulled the fire extinguishers off the walls at the last dance there. So Sam helped

Martin make a deal and they are going to have a barbecue and dance party in the field, not just with tennis club members, but with all the local teenagers invited. The tennis club will pay for all the food and a band and whatever else.

Marianne and I are going shopping again tomorrow. I want something even more amazing than the green dress. I wonder if maybe one day, if I don't yell or cry or make a fool of myself for maybe a year, then Martin might like me 'in that way'. I'd rather a year of thinking about him than a year of thinking about the King Rat.

I wonder if Martin would have kissed me?

7 AUGUST

OK, I may be hallucinating or I may be crazy or just over-reacting, or, in fact I may be all three, *but* Marianne might have guessed how I feel about her brother. When I was deciding whether to buy this amazing top in white or red, Marianne said (*way* too casually), 'Martin's favourite colour is red.' Which was the colour I turned right there in the changing room. 'Really,' I said (equally fake-casual) and then I bought the red one and nothing more was said, or not said, or something. God, I'm *SOOOOOO* confused! Anyway there are only a couple of days to go until what people are calling the Horse Field Party.

9 AUGUST

Charlie's back!!!! I hadn't checked my e-mail for weeks because of everything that was going on, so it was a total surprise. She was just sitting in the kitchen playing with Mikey when I got in from the shop. We talked *ALL* evening and half the night, as she stayed over. It turned out that my summer was way more eventful than hers, even though we'd both expected it to be the other way around. She did get to do loads of sailing and hang out with her Dad, which has made her really happy. Her Dad's girlfriend is expecting a baby and she's freaking out about that. Now that I'm cool with my new brother or sister (I think I felt different about it after Feather died) I was able to help her get a handle on it, tell her that it might be an OK thing.

She's so excited to meet Marianne. I didn't let her in on how I feel about Martin and I must admit that I'm a little nervous that he might fall for Charlie because she's so blonde and even more stunning looking with the tan she picked up over the summer. Still, I'm just so happy that she's back. Tomorrow night is the party!!!

10 AUGUST

What I said at the start of the summer, I take it all back, good stuff *does* happen these days. And if you are reading this in the twenty-third century let me tell you that amazing things can happen to you too.

The party was incredible: great barbecue, live band, and more people than you'd ever get at Club Havana. I made sure I looked gorgeous, and we got ready at my place so Marianne and Charlie could start to get to know each other. We all danced together and then Pete and Marianne went off to 'get more food', holding hands.

Martin disappeared soon after and I couldn't see Charlie either so I resigned myself to the fact that they might be off kissing somewhere, thinking it was my own fault as I didn't tell her that I liked him. I felt so hurt, and so stupid that I started to make my way across the field so I could get home and let it all out. Just then, the tennis club owner started to talk over the microphone, thanking people who made the night possible and all that usual stuff.

Suddenly, out of nowhere, Pete and Marianne pounced on me and started to walk me back round to the party.

Pete said, 'No princess, no more running off and doing crazy stuff, you are needed right here.'

I didn't have the words to explain what was going on, why I wanted to flee, and it wasn't until we got to the stage that I saw that Martin up there. He had taken the mike and was saying how great it was to have everyone there and how it was such a great chance for all the young people in the neighbourhood to get to know each other. I started to hope that maybe he hadn't gone off with Charlie.

I was still in a bit of an emotional funk, so his words sounded kind of far away and echoey, 'I want to thank my sister Marianne, our friends Pete and Sam, and particularly another friend of ours. This friend is so brave, smart, inspiring and funny that without her this summer would never have been the same.'

Was it me he was talking about? I *so* wanted it to be me.

With that, Martin said, 'Tammy, I have a gift for you, something that you deserve more than anyone else on the planet, and not just because you both have my favourite colour hair,' then he jumped from the stage and took me by the hand. Out from behind the stage walked Charlie leading Copper Girl who had a huge gold bow on her bridle. Martin took the reins from Charlie, and handed them to me.

With no microphone, he whispered in my ear, 'It's an honour to present you with your first horse, but this is on condition that you allow me to teach you to jump her.'

'Deal!' was all I could squeak out, before Martin landed this huge, amazing kiss on me. I don't know if it was seconds or minutes later, but I then looked around and saw everyone at the party clapping and laughing.

Martin and I walked Copper Girl back to her stable, and stayed a lot longer than was needed to settle her!

I can't believe it, I get Martin *and* Copper Girl all in one night!

'Guess the top worked,' Marianne winked at me as I left with Martin walking me home.

I have been awake for two hours now and I'm sure I won't sleep for days. I am happier than I have ever been in my entire life.

24
SEPTEMBER

Once school started I didn't really have enough time to write in this. Things have calmed down a lot, but in a good way.

I still get up to ride at six and then help out in the stables before school. It's amazing getting to see Martin every morning, even though we only have time to steal a few hugs and kisses. He calls it his 'school fuel', and says that kissing me makes the day feel easier. He is *so* romantic I won't even start with that. Sometimes I open my schoolbag to find a cute little note or a cookie or something that he's slipped in there.

After school on Mondays and Wednesdays I work in the shop until dinnertime. Every other weekday I can go to the stables once my homework is finished. I am now really good at riding; I can even jump small jumps. I chose not to go back to dancing and I don't really miss it as now there are so many teenagers up at the stables. Sam has worked out a whole volunteer system and the stables now do private lessons too.

Mum and I both work in the shop on Saturday mornings and then we meet Dad and Mikey in town and do some shopping and go to a gallery or a museum. I know that sounds kind of boring, but I really feel good about it, although I know it will have to stop once the baby arrives at Christmas.

On Saturday night the whole gang goes to a dance or round to Pete's house where we sit around in the huge kitchen, playing music and just having a laugh. His mum is cool and lets us do that without coming in all the time and wanting to make us tea. Of course, when we want tea we go round to Mrs Miggs. I feel like she's my granny too and she comes around with Martin and Marianne to have tea with our family every now and then.

A couple of times Martin and I have just gone for a

long walk or sat on our own talking in the stables. Last week he took me to see a live band. It was kind of embarrassing the way Dad fussed, but Martin thought it was great that Dad gets concerned for me, and the gig was AMAZING.

I feel like I'm pouring all this out like a list, it's just that now I'm more into living life than writing in this and complaining. The best thing is that now when I feel bad about something I say it instead of bottling it up and then getting depressed or letting it all burst out of me days later. Even when things go wrong, like when I caught hell for not doing my chemistry homework, and when Charlie thought I had said something about her that I didn't, I feel like there's enough good things to make it all safe. Charlie now knows that I didn't say anything and it was just Ester stirring it. Also, I remembered that I need to get good chemistry grades to become a vet, so I copped on to that one pretty swiftly (and now I'm Miss Carey's favourite!)

Martin has a new horse that someone found wandering starving on the motorway. He called him 'Pete', just to make Pete ridiculously happy. We picked 'Pete' up in the horsebox that Adie swapped for the Austin Page stuff. Adie has started calling in some afternoons and doesn't mind getting dirty mucking out stalls. She says she doesn't want another horse, she just wants to be around people who talk about other things than cars and skiing and holiday homes. She is really turning out to be OK now that she's stopped hanging out with Johnny and Doris. I'm going to ask her to come out with us all next Saturday.

On Sunday morning I mind Mikey while Mum and Dad do other stuff. Mum is back to her usual self and is more fun again. As Hellie (who came back two days after the Horse Field party), Charlie and Marianne come around for girl time, it's usually pretty fun. Mikey's walking is getting so much better and he is starting to talk so you can actually get what he's saying. Me and the girls all do songs and dances for him that we make up, and he *way* prefers our versions to the TV versions.

Then after Sunday lunch we all meet up again at the stables including Pete, Martin and Sean, who is now going out with Hellie and who (like Adie) turned out to be OK. Another friend of Pete's has started to show up which is making Charlie happy as she thinks he's fun. Last week we locked up early and all went to see a movie together.

I feel relaxed every day now, like life is making sense finally.

I can't believe that things can change so much in one summer. I thought that things were getting worse while really they were just getting different. I must remember that for the next time my life starts to grow in ways I don't yet understand.

Last night, sitting down with cups of tea to watch a cop show with Mum, she mentioned that the new baby will be a little girl.

'Let's call her Rose, after Granny,' I said, not expecting to be listened to.

At that moment Dad joined us. He smiled and nodded at Mum.

'Rose it is,' they said.

I know that Rose will be wonderful. I'll sing 'Yellow Bird' to her, and one day tell her this story.

**Hope you enjoyed Tammy's story,
now meet Tia in *Blue Lavender Girl***

DAY 6

This morning the post arrived after Mum and Dad had left for work. I read my end-of-year report and binned it. I know they won't ask. I used to get really good grades, As and Bs, and now I do really badly. I just can't be bothered. Anyway, don't need to think about it for another six months at least.

Parent-teacher meetings are in the bag. When my folks get the letter from the school asking why they weren't there, I say that I *definitely* told them about it last week. They know they forget about a lot of things when it comes to me and they feel guilty. They say they'll call in and talk to my teachers at some other time, but they never do (luckily for me!)

I think they peaked with my brother Aidan, I'm like

that second Mars Bar when you are full from the first one – OK, but not really worth it.

LATER

Mum and Dad have either

a) found my report in the bin

b) had a phone call

c) heard something on the radio about teenagers

d) decided my frozen pizza pockets for dinner were so bad that I must be evil …

Or anyway something has made them feel like making a decision about me.

Now I have three days to come up with a 'constructive and educational' plan for the summer or I am being sent to Aunt Maisie's for six weeks.

Aunt Maisie is a proper aunt, she buys me things, leaves me alone when I need it, doesn't ask awkward questions, talks to me, doesn't boss me about … did I mention she buys me things?

She is more fun than the rest of us put together and being with her instead of Mum and Dad would be bliss. BUT I couldn't stand to live in the countryside.

Mum says it's not the middle of nowhere (but it is) and that there is plenty to do. There is plenty to do if you are a granny, not if you are a teenager. I do not consider making rag dolls from old socks to be a 'fun activity', even if I did love it when I was seven. Anyway, it doesn't matter, I'm not going. I'm off to talk to Kira's Mum, she's a genius at coming up with stuff to get me and Dee off the hook with our folks.

DAY 7

FACT: I am now just about angry enough to do something reckless, but too angry to think what that might be. If not even Kira's mum is on my side, then it's safe to say that everyone is against me.

Kira was sitting there too and we were all drinking chamomile tea because they had just read up about it. While Kira's mum said, 'Tia, I think it would be a really good idea for you to get away for a while,' Kira was nodding like she was the wise woman of the west or whatever.

Then they both started this double-attack about me not being happy. Well, show me anyone who is happy! They are not even happy, they've just got more feel-good sayings and CDs than the rest of us.

Really.

I called Dee and said that if I can get out of this Aunt Maisie plan then we can both go into town this weekend and hang out at the market stalls and see if we can pretend we are sixteen and get jobs. She said that she was hanging out with Timmy this weekend, except that it took her half an hour to say it because she kept going on about all the cool things he said about her.

I called Aidan and he was out.

INTERESTING INFO: If you get my Dad away from my Mum you can sometimes encourage him to have an independent thought. But the plan was bigger than the both of us and he said that he and Mum would visit every second weekend, which for some bizarre reason was supposed to make me feel better.

No-one wants me here.

Well FINE!

I will probably be dead in two days anyway from having eaten nothing but cornflakes. I even had to make milk out of yogurt and water tonight, which doesn't really work.

DAY 8

I'm glad I didn't waste brain cells thinking of anything else to do for the summer, because I just found out that I'm going to Aunt Maisie's anyway. She always comes here so I've never seen her place. Mum tells me it's a large cottage in its own grounds, but if she thinks that will change me into one of those *Pride and Prejudice* girls she's very much mistaken.

I'm sort of relieved though, because I hate everyone right now, but I won't let them know that.

I need to use every minute I have to make it so they won't go into my room while I'm away. That way they can't pull another stunt like the salmon-coloured, flowered wallpaper that appeared when I was off on the weekend school trip to that farm. I am going to push all the mess near the door so it's impossible to get through.

I put all my favourite clothes into a big suitcase and then took them all out again deciding to wash everything first in case she doesn't have a washing machine. I know she will, I just … God, I don't know.

I went around to meet Kira and Dee at the burger place, but they sounded worse than my mother. They kept saying that I'd have a good time and they wish they were going and that I might find a boyfriend there. I told them I don't want a boyfriend, but I didn't say that I didn't want to be all ridiculous like they are over the Timmys. The other guy's name is not actually Timmy I just can't be bothered learning any more names of guys they like, so from now on they are all just Timmy. Once we are all ancient and they get to the altar, then I'll learn the guys' real names.

I didn't even get to say goodbye properly because Dee's brother's friends arrived in, and this needed the girls' full attention in case things don't work out with the current round of Timmys.

I had to ask Dad for money and he said 'How much?' That bugs me because he should really have thought of it and then he should have given me more